A Foreign Job

The flat rent was costing too much and he was contemplating moving back to Birmingham. Dave had been told by one of his army buddies that there were many security jobs in London. He had tried several jobs but could not settle to the environment. He kept giving advice that was rarely taken and was wondering whether the local crooks had an influence in the security companies. He was never on duty when robberies happened. Even though he changed jobs these breaches of security were happening all the time. He was not going to fight organized crime on his own so here he was deciding his future. It was time to think of returning to Birmingham. His sister and mother still lived there. It would mean having to look for a new job and maybe he would have to go abroad.

One of his jobs had been as a bouncer at a night club. During the evening he and his mate were persuading men and women that they were too drunk to enjoy the club. The drug addicts were obviously not drunk but acting irrationally. Drugs were becoming popular on the street and reefers were in abundant supply. Dave became pally with the night club owner and warned him of these new developments. These druggies could be uncontrollable and dealing with them could be hazardous. The owner was aware of the problem and invited Dave to sit in the club when he had free time and observe the patrons. Dave would sit with a free beer and watch as he saw drugs being circulated. The manager would be informed of the pushers and at some later date the police would be told. This did not eradicate the problem but slowed down the trade.

The manager told Dave that some people were becoming suspicious of the club informing the police about their trade. Dave could still come to the club and have his free beer but information would not be passed to the police for a while. Dave understood the situation and would have loved to issue these people with a bit of punishment but understood the problem was too big for him.

Late one afternoon he was sitting having a cold beer when a pretty young lady sat at his table. She was not one of the regular 'girls'; they all knew him. Dave was on the defensive; what was a good looking young lady doing sitting with him?

"Do I have to buy my own drink?"

"Well, I will get you a drink but I am not sure who is paying. I am not sure what you have to sell but I am not interested and could not afford it anyway. You are an attractive young lady and I think you might be in the wrong place."

"Oh, I am not in the wrong place and I am not selling myself. I have come with a proposition, one that could increase your bank balance. Now can I have a drink?"

That was of interest as Dave's bank balance was almost nil. He went to the bar with a puzzled look on his face.

"Well, here is your drink; it is only a soft drink as I think young ladies should not drink booze in the afternoon."

"Well, so far you are living up to expectations. Do you remember working with a Russian called Boris?"

"Yes, a nice guy too good for our line of work. I am sure his main job was not as a security man."

"Boris is not his real name but he is one of our group. He tells us that you were a sniper in the Korean War. How would you like to earn some money by shooting an evil man?"

"Wow, in one sentence you have probably increased my blood pressure. One minute, let me get this straight, you want me to shoot an unarmed man, I assume he will be unarmed. You want me to kill him and not just maim him."

"Yes, that is correct we assume he will be unarmed. We definitely want him killed."

Dave was born in Birmingham before the war and he spent his teenage years with his parents. As his father was not around much, most of his childhood was spent with his mother. There was serious bombing in the

Birmingham area but for children life went on. Playing in the street and going to the bomb shelter when the siren sounded was part of a normal life. His mother would not let him be evacuated and at fifteen he was employed in a foundry. The bombs were still being dropped on Birmingham but the foundry was not hit. The Home Guard had him training with them and they noticed he was a good shot. One sergeant told him that when he was conscripted he should let them know he could use a rifle and could shoot anything. Dave did not want to be conscripted but it was inevitable. He was worried that if he spoke up about his rifle expertise he would be picked on. One or two of the Home Guard had warned him about bullying in the army.

His job in the foundry was dirty and in a way he was not unhappy to be conscripted. The workers were friendly and there were lots of crude jokes but he could not get rid of the metal smell; it seemed to be in his nose wherever he went. He had a girlfriend for a while but she 'packed him in'. In a way he was not too upset. She always wanted to do things he disliked and he always wanted to do things she disliked.

He was sent a letter that instructed him that he should report to Snow Hill Station at such and such a time on a specific date. His foreman at the foundry was unhappy to let him go, because Dave was a good worker. The workers gave him a good send off before he left. The reception was at a local pub and Dave left before getting drunk. He knew many of the others would get sloshed and he wanted to be long gone before that happened.

The day approached and his mother cried all the way to the station; she was losing her son to the army but it was lucky there was no current war. At the station he met several other conscripts and they were all put on a train, destination Hereford. There were introductions all around and they were from different parts of Birmingham and two from Smethwick.

Dave loved the seats on the train and thought he would fall asleep but the scenery was too interesting. Most of it was green fields; he had never before been out of Birmingham. He saw cows, sheep and horses running freely. The only horses he had ever seen were pulling milk or bread carts. The train did not stop before Hereford but there were lots of interesting villages on the way. At Hereford station they were picked up by a couple of lorries and taken somewhere in the countryside to an army camp. They were lined up and given ill-fitting uniforms. Dave hated his uniform. It made him itch but at least the boots fitted his large feet.

After a few days marching and being told how to hold their rifles, they were ushered to the firing range. Dave had no problem, the Home Guard had given him plenty of experience but some of his mates had no idea. The sergeant showed them how to load and fire their rifles and decided that he would watch each man. Dave was near the end of the line and was hoping many of his mates would not be firing with him. They were dreadful shots. The targets were rarely hit and loading and unloading seemed to escape some of the men. Finally it came to Dave's turn. He lay down, loaded his rifle and hit the bull's eye first time. The sergeant instructed him to stand and asked if he could do that in a standing position. Dave reloaded, fired and hit the bull. Now he had to take a kneeling position and hit the bull again. The sergeant suspended the operation.

"Where did you learn to shoot like that?"

"Well I had some training with the Home Guard."

The sergeant raised his eyebrows when the Home Guard was mentioned but didn't comment.

"Everyone, watch this man load and unload his rifle and I want you all to follow him."

Watching one of their own seemed to have a beneficial effect with only two men fumbling the process. Dave was instructed to help these two, it turned out they were both left handed. Then Dave did the process left handed and they followed with success. He explained to the sergeant that he was ambidextrous but he preferred to fire right handed. The sergeant explained ambidextrous to the other soldiers and then told Dave to fire first right handed then left handed. Dave's left handed shots hit the target but not as well as his right handed ones. The sergeant explained that if this man was injured on his right side he could still operate on his left side. Dave was hoping never to be injured on either side.

He was a natural and explained to his troop to take firing easily, not to worry if they missed the target but to understand why. Within a couple of sessions the whole troop were regularly hitting the target. The sergeant was happy and said that this troop of conscripts was the best he had ever seen. An officer came to watch them on the firing range and he picked out Dave.

"You will be leaving us and going to Japan."

"Yes, sir, where is Japan?"

'I will get you a map from the library but be ready to leave tomorrow or the next day. Just pack your basic kit. You will get a new one when you get to Japan."

Dave knew of the war with Japan but his geography gave him little idea of the location. His school studies had concentrated on the Empire and everything except America was a big unknown. His mates were poring over the maps and someone asked the important question.

"How are you going to get there?"

This set the whole troop discussing various possibilities and someone suggested they bet on the possible routes. They were all studying the maps. Dave was not allowed to bet as he would be gone when the route was finalized. Lots of discussion ended with four routes favoured and one totally discounted. If he was going to the Far East via Russia everyone would get their money back. He could go via the RAF through Egypt and India, he could go by air through America, he could go by sea through the Suez Canal or he could go via South Africa to Ceylon (now Sri Lanka) and then to Japan. There were multiple other suggestions but they all agreed to bet on the four options. Internally, Dave was laughing at himself being like a race horse. He was looking forward to the journey by whatever route the army chose.

None of the routes was correct but his first departure was using the RAF to go through Cairo on to India then Hong Kong. From Hong Kong he was to go by sea to Japan. His mates could only have known his first trip by RAF to Egypt. He assumed some of them would have won some money. His planned route was okay by him but then he had no say.

The whole squad wished him the best of luck. Some wished they were going. The next day he was transported to an airfield near Coventry. He was not told the name of the airfield but he saw Birmingham and the ruins of Coventry Cathedral. It was obviously east of Coventry. Not having flown before he was a little apprehensive, nay very apprehensive. At the airport he met three other soldiers from different parts of Britain and one was shivering at the thought of flying. This group all shook hands and all agreed no one had flown before. They were lined up and an RAF officer inspected their rifles to make sure they were unloaded. He told them they would be in the back of the plane with no windows and they would have a safety harness to their seats. There was nothing to worry about but tell four men nothing to worry and they were still worried.

Take off was smooth and during the flight there were introductions all around. The shiverer was from Scotland but he soon calmed down and said he was enjoying the flight. They all decided they had been picked as they were good shots. The other three had not seen maps and Dave was explaining where Japan was located. They were all surprised that it was closer to China than America and they were all thinking of Pearl Harbour.

They did not see much of Egypt. On landing they were taken to the mess for food and then shown a tent where they would sleep the night. They were given two free beers and some 'smokes' and were instructed not to leave the tent as they did not know the password. Dave explained this must be a very restricted area in the desert. The next day they were on the plane again, this time to Calcutta. Again they saw nothing of India, their accommodation was on the airfield. Leaving the plane they noticed it was hot and humid, there was also a peculiar smell that had lots of crude comments and explanations.

Dave felt they were like pawns in a big game, at least they were told next stop was Hong Kong and then by sea to Japan. In India they were supplied with tropical uniforms and they were all happy not to wear long trousers. The Scotsman asked for a kilt but none were available. They at least received two free beers. The next day after breakfast they were ushered onto the back of the plane with no windows but they had a cold box with two beers each. Someone in the army was thinking about them. One of the flight crew warned it would be a long flight and not to drink their beers all at once.

They landed in Hong Kong and immediately the smell hit them. This was a different smell than Calcutta but similar in many ways. The general opinion was that it was human although it was expressed more crudely. Unloading themselves from the plane they felt the humidity. They were taken to a barracks in Kowloon and they seemed to be getting used to the smell. The food in the canteen was good and they received another couple of beers. It was good the beers were free as none of them had any cash. Many soldiers came and shook their hands; it seemed their prowess with guns was well known. This was a nice barracks with comfortable beds and they all had a good sleep.

Leaving the barracks the next day they were taken to the harbour. There seemed to be people everywhere and the road was crammed with bicycles, cars and lorries. There were pedestrians dodging the traffic and horns seemed to be continually blasted in unison. At the dock everything seemed to get back to normal and they lined up to board their next transport. To their surprise it was a freighter. They were expecting a battleship or a cruiser but this ship had been commandeered by the army to supply Japan. They had a four-berth cabin and the only other soldiers on the ship were two officers who had a cabin each. One of the crew instructed them how to use the facilities and the meal times. He said he was happy to have four hot shots on board as there were pirates all around the coast. The Scotsman thought he was joking but the sailor said he was deadly serious.

As the ship left the harbour they were allowed on deck and they were all amazed at the number and size of the boats there. The smell receded as they left the harbour and then the swell took over. None of them had ever been to sea and all of them were feeling unwell. The next two meals were almost avoided. Dave was affected more than the others and he decided he had to do something to take his mind off the rocking of the ship. He could not get used to the motion and so he had a sleepless night.

One of the crew suggested he face the wind and jog on the spot. If he kept his mind on the jogging and how tired he felt it would take his mind off the queasy feeling he had. At first Dave thought it would not work but he had to try anything. He had to concentrate on keeping upright and staying on one spot; it was working. Inside the cabin there was the claustrophobic effect but jogging helped. After a couple of days the four stopped trying to move with the ship's motion and just let it happen. They were getting their sea legs and eating better than before.

One day, one of the officers, a captain, asked what they would like to do. One fellow suggested they shoot at a target. Another suggested they make a target and trail it after the ship. The ship's captain said there was some spare packing case wood and they could make a target with that. One of the crew was a carpenter so they set about making a floating target. It was a painted sheet attached to a square surround. They all forgot about the motion of the ship. A long rope was found to attach the target and the ship. When the target was launched everyone was cheering and the soldiers let the officer have the first shot. With the motion of the ship he missed. The four soldiers were the next to shoot. The first three hit the target but not the bull. Dave was the last to shoot and he had judged the wind and the motion. He hit the bull to great applause. The ship's captain gave him a glass of rum and Dave said he had never drunk spirits. With his mates and the crew shouting, he had to down the rum. The burning in his throat had him vowing not to try neat rum again.

Dave tried to find out from the officers where they were going and what they would be doing. They admitted they knew very little except that there were many prisoner of war in camps dotted all over Japan. The Americans seemed to be in control although there were plenty of Australian troops stationed there. Dave was happy there would not be any fighting. He could not really imagine a prisoner of war camp, he had not seen the recent newsreels. In fact he had not seen any news for weeks. He was missing home but seeing new things all the time.

They docked in Yokohama and there were ships of every size in the port. The dock seemed to be full of soldiers, mainly American but no Japanese. They boarded American lorries called trucks and they were transported to a camp. Along the way Dave could see Japanese staring at them. These people were very different and he could not judge whether they were welcoming them or the reverse. The mess was very welcoming and again they had a good meal with two complimentary beers. They were shown to their quarters and told after breakfast they would be informed where they were going. His mates were all anxious to talk about what could happen but Dave could not get used to no rocking motion. He had another sleepless night.

Before breakfast they were issued with new uniforms, one for winter and one for summer. They were told that summer could be hot and winter could be cold. The winter kit was interesting as they had thick socks, gloves and thermal underwear. The Scotsman said he did not need underwear under his kilt, unfortunately he was not issued with a kilt. His mates thought they really did not want to see under his kilt. After breakfast they were told they would be guarding prison camps. These were full of Japanese soldiers many of whom had not surrendered and so did not like being locked up. Dave and his mates would be stationed in a tower overlooking the camp and could shoot any prisoner who was attempting to escape. The officer explained these Japanese soldiers did not understand surrender. The four looked at each other; they had only ever shot at targets. They all expressed the opinion that they would prefer to be anywhere else (in rather cruder terms).

The camp where Dave was stationed was shared by British, Australian and New Zealand troops. Everyone was very friendly and Dave found the Antipodeans very open. They would tell you their life story if you had time to listen. Within days Dave was close to two or three. They told him a lot about Australia and New Zealand. The camp had two towers and one of his mates manned the tower at the other side of the camp. Being new they had night duty. There were lights that scanned the camp but at any particular time parts of the perimeter fence would be in darkness. For the first two nights there was an officer present in Dave's tower but on the third night there was none and Dave had a problem staying awake. As he awoke from a mini-nap he thought he saw a figure on the fence. He fired and a body dropped to the ground. He could tell it was a body as the lights came on and focused on it. He could see other figures running away. An officer came and congratulated him and said they would write a short report.

"The army wants to know about every spent bullet."

Dave was thinking it was a good job they did not want to know about every penny spent. The report was short and later Dave heard the prisoner was still alive and was wounded in the shoulder. His friends in the canteen were congratulating him; many said he should shoot more as they had seen released prisoners of war.

Starving British, Australian and New Zealand soldiers and many of his mates hated the Japanese. The camp became quieter and after a few weeks Dave was moved to a more 'problematic' camp. This was larger and seemed to be under the control of the Americans. There were some British officers but most of the guards were American and the camp commander was American. The food in the mess was much better but Dave did not like the beer. He thought at least one beer tasted like a weak soap solution. Generally, the beer was so cold there was almost no taste. The choice of food particularly meat was fantastic, it was his first taste of salami and he loved it. He had only eaten turkey once before and the only thing not so good were the sausages. There were cheeses of all kinds and Dave was thinking he would get fat on this food.

He had his allowance of British beer and cigarettes (although he did not smoke) and he would trade his 'smokes' for chewing gum and Hershey bars. American chocolate was different to Cadbury's and he liked the taste. The soldiers were from all over the States and he was always talking to the officers. The first time he went to dinner in their mess he saw a free seat at a table with black soldiers. As he went to sit they politely told him to sit at another table. He sat next to a white American soldier who told him, "We do not like them sitting with us and they don't like us sitting with them." Dave thought he did not understand; they were all soldiers in the same army.

He was on day duty which he preferred and some of the American officers were quite friendly and Dave learned a bit about America. He was chatting with an officer when in broad daylight a prisoner started to scale the fence.

"Shoot that man, shoot to kill."

Dave did just that and the prisoner fell to the ground. Dave knew he was dead as the bullet had pierced his skull. The officer was jumping up and down with glee telling Dave he would get a medal. Dave was not feeling too good but he had a report to write. He was summoned before the commander who pinned a medal on his chest. He also received a glass of scotch on the 'rocks'. The commander (a general) asked what Dave would like. He said he was not keen on shooting unarmed soldiers so if they set up a firing range and let the prisoners watch that might deter them from trying to escape.

"Brilliant idea, but you must appreciate that these prisoners want to escape and we still regard them as the enemy. I agree no soldier likes to shoot an unarmed soldier but if they are trying to escape that is what we have to do."

The general was pleased with the firing exhibition and Dave kept hitting the bull. The American soldiers were cheering his every shot. He could see the prisoners were enjoying the exhibition and he was hoping that might put them off escaping. In the next few weeks the camp was quiet and Dave had a few drinks with the general. The general drank whisky and bourbon and Dave started to like bourbon. Dave was telling the general about England and the general was telling him about America. The general admitted he could not have the same chat with an American private.

Word was coming through that there was a war in Korea and Dave was getting very new news. The general had maps of Korea and was showing the allied forces retreating much to his displeasure. It seemed inevitable that Dave would be ordered to Korea. The general told him he was to join the Gloucester regiment and made sure he had the best American transport. When Dave left the general was at the airport to see him off.

Arriving in Korea he realised this was real war. Everything seemed to be in confusion and it took a while for Dave to be united with his regiment. He sat for a couple of days before his orders came. All he could gather was that his regiment was holding a hill and would be attacked by Chinese troops. Dave's job as a sniper was to shoot any Chinese he thought was an officer. Dave thought that was better than shooting enlisted men. There was no need to report every bullet spent as he was going to be using lots of ammunition. It was impressed on him that the Chinese were out to kill soldiers of his regiment so he should have no second thoughts about killing them. He was also told to change position regularly so that the Chinese would not get a fix on his position.

He had no time to set up his position before the Chinese were attacking. His targets were five hundred yards away and he had no problem hitting them. He was so involved in firing that an officer had to tell him to change position. Now the assault was in full swing and he was killing as many Chinese as he could. His rifle was getting hot. His regiment was ordered to retreat and although Dave wanted to stay he was ordered to retreat. He had heard a few bullets pass his head and he realised that there must be a sniper targeting him. That night he slept well and in the morning he wanted to join the slaughter. He had no idea how the battle was going but he just kept firing. The targets were too numerous but he no longer regarded them as human. After a few days they were relieved and Dave was exhausted. He was still a conscript and was hoping when his time was up they would let him go. He still did not know what happened to his regiment but was glad to be evacuated from the front line.

The army finally caught up with Dave's time and shipped him back to England to be demobbed. Suddenly he had an urge to sign up for a couple of years. He knew he could not decide where he would be posted but he thought he would try his luck. One thing he had to do was to talk to someone who knew him well. He chose his grandfather.

"Well son, I was in the First World War but I never fired a gun, I was driving a food lorry, I was lucky. After what I saw I think I could have shot Germans but I never got the chance."

Dave said, "Actually I killed many men but the only one I regret was the Japanese prisoner who was trying to escape. I could have shot him in the leg and he would have fallen from the wire, but I was ordered to kill. All the others were different, they were trying to kill me and my mates. What surprised me was that I could sleep after a day's shooting."

His grandfather said, "You must have been mentally exhausted. I agree the prisoner was different but when you are in the army an order is an order."

Dave said, "Yes that man comes back occasionally in nightmares, I am apologizing to him. I now understand a bit about Japanese culture and he had to try to escape but his death is still with me. Should I sign up for another tour?"

His grandfather said, "I don't think there is a war on at the moment but you are now used to army life and there will be no surprises. My advice is to sign up for a short time and see how it goes; I think it would be preferable to the foundry."

Dave said, "You are right there, I cannot imagine going back to that factory. I never felt clean when I was working there."

Signing up was a difficult task for Dave but the more he thought about the alternatives he realised he did not want back to go to the past. He signed up and was sent to Germany, to the British zone. There were still some prison camps and of course he became a guard and hated it. He requested a transfer and because of his Army record he was assigned to a patrol of the border. Germany had a new government but the border between the old British zone and the Russian zone was a hostile place still patrolled by the British. Dave often had eye to eye contact with Russian troops on the border. Occasionally they would shout pleasantries at each other and on other occasions insults. Some Germans had taught them Russian insults and the Russians obviously knew some English. Sitting in a jeep eight hours a day with three other soldiers either builds friends or enemies. Luckily for Dave he had three good friends. They swapped stories and hopes for the future and of course dates when they would leave the army. One of his mates, Fred was from London and he planned to join a security company when he was free. He told them all there was plenty of work in London. He did warn they would not have guns unless they were delivering money to the Bank of England. At this stage Dave wanted to get rid of his gun. He was thinking seriously about what he would do when he left the army and Fred had given him an idea...

During his time in Germany Dave learnt a bit of German and made a few German friends. He enjoyed their food and beer and listened to their stories. He was interested in a German girl but she ran off with an American soldier so Dave resigned himself to a life of celibacy. Drinking with Germans introduced him to various beers; he enjoyed the beer although he was not a big drinker and rum was certainly not his drink. He also enjoyed their markets and he could see the devastation of bombing still visible years later as some of the markets were on bombed sites.

After leaving the army he went back to Birmingham to live with his mother and sister. His father had died during the war. His mother was not well and they were struggling to pay the rent even with his mother's pension. They applied for a council flat and with Dave's service record they were easily bumped to the front of the queue. Dave could find jobs in security but the pay was not too good. Patrolling shops or warehouses was easy but boring and Dave wanted more.

He contacted Fred and had a job as soon as he reached London and now he was sitting on a park bench with an attractive young lady.

"How would you like to earn some money by shooting an evil man?" she asked.

"I am not in the business of shooting men even evil ones, but tell me more."

"First of all if you succeed we will pay you five thousand pounds."

Suddenly Dave became more interested.

"Who are we?"

"That does not matter but are you interested?"

"Well, you have raised my interest but I may need a lot more detail."

"The man we want you to shoot is Russian and you will kill him in Russia."

Now Dave was intrigued.

"I have never been to Russia, and don't speak the language although I know a few words (Dave did not say most of them were bad). Who is this evil man and why is he evil?"

"He is a governor of an area east of Moscow. Under Stalin he rose to power by his ruthless treatment of fellow Russians. Stalin died in 1953 but he still wields a lot of power. He has had many men killed or thrown into prison and forced many women into prostitution. I want you to think on this and we can meet on this bench in two days. By the way do not try to follow me."

"I was not planning to so rest easy."

Dave went back to his flat and started to think five thousand pounds could solve a lot of his problems. He needed to help his mother and sister and would like a holiday. Could he shoot an unarmed man? He assumed the man would be unarmed. Then he remembered he had shot an unarmed Japanese soldier. He started to think of this man wielding lots of power; he was not a simple soldier more like a high ranking officer.

The only Russian he knew was Boris. He'd met him on a job protecting a warehouse. They chatted every night and Dave had no idea what was in the warehouse but all he had to do was patrol around the perimeter. Boris was a friendly man but he spoke little about his background or Russia. Thinking back, Boris seemed to be in charge. Dave now realised Boris obtained more information from him than he did from Boris. Now he started to wonder what was in that warehouse.

"Okay, young lady, I might be interested but I need a lot more information," said Dave.

"I will tell you my interest in eliminating this man. He had my father thrown in prison for a crime he did not commit. My father opposed this man and said he was corrupt. My father died in prison and then my mother committed suicide. I went to live with my uncle and later we escaped to the West."

"Okay, I can see your motive," said Dave.

The bit about her mother had Dave thinking of his own mother who was seriously ill.

"We know you know nothing about Russia and we would like to give you a holiday with Intourist, the government travel agency. We will pay for your holiday and give you spending money. You will visit Moscow, a place called Sochi and Leningrad. In the hotel in Sochi you will meet a lady who will give you more information."

"You mean I am going to get a week's holiday?"

"Actually it will be nine days, two in Moscow, five in Sochi and two in Leningrad."

"How do I pay for this holiday?"

"We will give you the money if you will seriously consider this proposition. We will meet in two days and I look forward to your answer. It is no use trying to follow me."

News from Birmingham was not good, Dave's mother was in hospital. His sister had told him not to worry and he told her he would be there in two days. If his mother died they would lose her pension and then it would be more important to have extra money. He was deciding he had to do this job but he had to know more about Sochi.

The next meeting was short and Dave agreed to go on holiday but he said there was a problem with his mother. He would have to go to Birmingham but would soon return to London.

"We know about the problem and you can delay your holiday, you have our sympathy. Here is the money for your trip. We will know when you make the booking, I hope it is soon."

"You people have certainly done your homework, now I have to catch a train. Try not to follow me."

Dave arrived in Birmingham and caught a bus straight to the hospital. He found his sister in the waiting room; she had obviously been crying. His mother had died a few hours before his arrival. They sat grieving in the waiting room before Dave could get his sister to go home. At home there was the obligatory cup of tea and then she told him that a strange man came up to her. He had a funny accent and expressed his condolences; he had given her an envelope addressed to Dave. She took it from her handbag and when Dave opened it he found one hundred pounds. He explained it was probably from one of his mates he had told his mother was sick.

Now he knew he was getting indebted to this group, whoever they were. He gave the money to his sister and told her to use it for funeral expenses and rent. She should make the arrangements and he would be back from London in a couple of days. He wanted to sit on the park bench and get more information but did not tell his sister that.

"You don't have to worry about a visa, Intourist will do all that. You can learn a little Russian but the people that matter will speak English. Moscow and Leningrad could be cold but Sochi could be warm. Go on all the trips offered but particularly the one to Georgia to see the locals dance. Try to remember the route and any buildings you see. Enjoy yourself. Don't get involved with the ladies in Moscow or Leningrad. They are not ours."

Dave was smiling to himself. Here was a young lady telling him to leave other ladies alone. Suddenly his interest in ladies was activated. Could he enjoy this holiday? At least he was not paying for it. He was starting to think about his travelling companions.

"Will I see you again?" asked Dave.

"Most certainly. I will need a report, verbal of course. I also want to know your impression of Russia."

The lady at Intourist was very happy he was taking the only trip currently available. She took his passport and told him to collect it with a visa in a couple of days. The agent had a few brochures about Russia and he took them. It was a little light reading with good pictures.

After a couple of days he collected his tickets and found he was flying from Gatwick.

Dave took the train and checked in at Gatwick and flew out to Moscow on Aeroflot. At Gatwick there had been a lady who gathered the group together to get to the boarding terminal. Everything at the airport went smoothly and he was in a happy mood. He had a window seat and this was the first time he had flown on a commercial plane and he had a view. The seat was a bit cramped for his body size but it was not a long flight. Landing at Sheremetyevo airport in Moscow the immigration officers were very polite and even smiled. Dave was not really expecting such a warm reception. His fellow passengers were a mixed group. There were several couples from Scotland, they were coal miners. There was a young fellow who had won a trip through some contest on Radio Moscow. There was one American couple and four English couples. He and the student were the only single people. Dave was now in observation mode and wanted to know more about these people. He was going to spend nine days with them.

They were checked into a large hotel and were given a schedule with a plan of the hotel and the surrounding area. He was given a rather large key and a room number on the sixth floor. His room was small but comfortable and he had his own toilet, shower and a good view. Actually he was expecting a bath but a shower was adequate. At the end of the hall was a little cubicle with an older lady, who was there to help solve any problems. Her English was not too good so he was happy he had no problems. After dropping his bag he went to dinner which was sort of self-service where you lined up and pointed to what you wanted. The meat on a skewer was good although he never found out what meat it was. The vegetables were not to his liking but the black bread with butter and a peculiar cheese were delicious. The coffee was like sludge. He was later to learn that it was goat cheese (he would eat plenty in the future) and he was better off with tea.

After dinner he went to the bar and ordered a beer. He sat at a table on his own. The waiter came and asked if he needed company but Dave said just a beer please. The beer was to his liking, it was very much like German beer. He sat quietly sipping it and was approached by several ladies but he waved them away. He was smiling at remembering his young lady's warning. The bar was on the top floor of the building and all the window seats were full but he was able to get a table with a view. At night the city seemed not to be well lit but he thought he could see the Kremlin. He had done a bit of reading about Moscow. He also took a professional look at the security. There was one policeman in uniform but several men keeping an eye on proceedings. There were several drunken patrons and they were not all men. After a couple of beers he decided to retire. The lady in the kiosk said good night and asked if he was alone. She was keeping an eye on the comings and goings. He smiled and found a very welcome bed; he had a very good sleep.

He awoke early in the morning and decided to go for a walk before breakfast. The air was cool and he could see his breath. As he left the hotel he saw guards and they smiled at him. Around the hotel everything was clean and tidy. He decided to walk towards a block of flats. As he approached the flats he could see large lagged pipes and one or two flats with washing on the balcony. At this point he decided to turn back as he had not realised how cold he was.

One of the hotel guards saw him rubbing his hands as he entered the hotel and asked if he wanted vodka. Dave had never tried vodka before but thought it inappropriate that early in the morning. The guard obviously thought otherwise. Breakfast of eggs and bacon was good but the little sausages were like bullets. He decided on tea rather than coffee and it was a good choice. The black bread and butter made this breakfast worth the effort. The other couples were a bit bleary eyed and he sat with an English couple. He found that the wife was Russian and her English was good. He asked her about the pipes and she told him they were hot water or steam to heat the batteries in the flats. Dave frowned when she said batteries so she corrected herself and said radiators.

"We cannot discuss politics but I wish I had your dialect, we could have some fun with the security."

All this time her husband had been silent but suddenly said, "Wherm yo from, Brumigem?"

Now Dave had a good laugh and realised his Birmingham accent had been recognized. The lady explained that she was going to visit her sisters while her husband would take the city tour. After the tour he would try to find the address written in both English and also with Cyrillic script. Dave would be very welcome to join him. The Metro stations were highlighted and Dave and the husband were given the rough English translation. This lady called Olga said they should enjoy the city tour; it was the first time her husband had been in Moscow.

The city tour was very interesting with lots of magnificent buildings to see. Dave thought that many needed a paint job but the churches were beautiful. Some of the church domes were in different colours and beautifully shaped. They were shown the Kremlin but told at this time they could not enter. Stalin and Lenin's tomb were interesting as the guards had a magnificent high stepping drill. Dave watched these guards with interest. The highlight was Red Square with the most fantastic church at one end. Dave and Trevor (the husband of Olga) asked to be left in the city centre and pointed to the nearest Metro station. They studied the map and showed the destination at the payment booth. They were surprised at how cheap the tickets were. They had to change trains at a central station and that meant changing platforms. Dave could not get over the beauty of the stations; he was used to the London Underground. The stations had statues and paintings. The only decoration on the London underground was the adverts and the platforms had a very sombre look. The timing of the trains was lit up at the end of the platform and the trains were on time again which was another plus for the Metro.

At the central station they went from platform to platform but could not find the correct train. It was frustrating but still enjoyable. Dave was enjoying the escalators with a lady at the end telling people what to do. Finally they had to ask directions from a policeman. The man smiled and took them to the correct platform. In his best English he said thank you as they were thanking him.

The train was not crowded and Dave was interested in how the people were dressed. There were some very good looking young ladies and most of the men were well dressed. They alighted at the station written on the paper but now had to find the address. At one of the kiosks they were directed in a direction but they decided to ask a policeman. He smiled and took them to the address. Dave was used to dealing with police but these two policemen had been smilers and very helpful, not like some English policemen he had known.

They were greeted at the door by Olga and her two sisters, Mila and Vlada. There was also a young boy called Leo (Leonid). The flat was small but the table was laid with all sorts of dishes and a bottle of vodka and a bottle of brandy. Dave was a bit embarrassed as he had not expected to be fed. Olga explained that her sisters rarely had visitors and they wanted to put on a good show. Both sisters were scientists but they could not say where they worked; it was a secret. They apologized for not having beer but vodka and local brandy were almost as cheap. Olga told her husband and Dave to eat heartily or the sisters would feel that the food was not good enough. Dave tucked in and the vodka and water went down well. He ate the pickles and meat slices that were different to ham or salami, they called it *kielbasa*. Leo sat in the corner studying these two new men. Dave had to give this lad something and as he felt in his pocket he found a penny, a threepenny bit and a sixpence. He gave them to Leo who smiled and showed his mother. Dave said to Olga it was all he could think of but she said he would treasure them.

The conversation was a bit stunted as the English of the sister was limited. They told him that they both went to Moscow State University. Olga explained that education was free and the bright ones went to university. She would have gone to university but escaped to the West. Her family was not rich but her parents were very keen on education. Dave was thinking what might have been if he had lived in this country. He had left school at fifteen and had never thought about going to university; he suddenly felt cheated. He learned a lot about living in Moscow, it was so different from England. Finally when it was time to go he had a kiss from both sisters and a wave from Leo. This had been a very unexpected day and the last few hours were all he could think of even outshining the Kremlin and Red Square.

These three sisters were beautiful and two of them had university degrees. He was treated as an honoured guest and could not get over the way they behaved. This was the first time he had been in the presence of beautiful educated women and he wanted it to happen again. He was amazed at how small the flat was and one person in the kitchen had to be a maximum. The ride back to the hotel on the Metro was a pleasure and he thanked Olga for a very entertaining afternoon.

Back at the hotel the guide gave them a list of instructions. They were to have their luggage outside their rooms at five a.m. and have breakfast at six a.m. Some of the people grumbled but it was no problem for Dave. He was still daydreaming about his afternoon.

In the early morning they were taken to the airport but the flight was delayed. They all retired to the coffee shop but were ushered out by the cleaner. This was not a happy set of tourists and the guide could only keep apologizing. Dave did not mind, he could get to know some of the passengers but he kept gravitating to Trevor and Olga. Olga said she was not surprised at the delay but Trevor was complaining about getting up so early. The flight to Sochi was quite short but they did not get to the hotel until late in the afternoon and they were all hungry. In the restaurant the dishes on offer were very interesting and different. Dave stood in front of a large white mass and asked what it was. The server spoke English and said it was Salo sometimes called Sala, it was pork fat. Dave declined that dish and took meat and vegetables on a skewer he assumed they had been cooked over an open flame. He was not used to barbecuing. They had black bread and butter so he was going to enjoy his meal. He refused the coffee and only had black tea. He thought the meat on the skewer was tough but tasty and he refused a sweet.

After his meal he retired to the bar even though he thought it was a bit early. The bar was almost empty but he could identify the security. The waiter with his beer did not ask if he wanted company but told him a lady might come later. This was good beer and seemed to be brewed locally. The view from this bar was not too good but he could see the sea, the Black Sea. During his second beer he was approached by a very good looking and well-endowed lady. He was about to wave her away but he thought of his instructions. Any way she was too good looking to reject her advances, even early in the day.

"Hello, Brummie, will you buy me a drink?"

"Yes, what would you like, beer vodka or wine? I recommend the beer, it is like German beer."

"No. I will have Champagne, we call it Champanska."

This was his contact but he was puzzled what he could say to her. She was good looking and very desirable and her English so far was good. He ordered the drink and waited.

"I know you are confused but after a couple of drinks we will leave and go for a drive. Do not worry this *Champanska* is diluted and I am a careful driver."

Dave could not take his eyes off this lady; if these were Russian women he could not get enough. They left the bar and went to the car park, the guards at the entrance were all smiling. Dave got into this small car, a make he did not recognize. He was surprised he had leg room.

"I am Mila and you are Dave. I want to show you some of our countryside."

Although Mila had an accent her English was clear. Dave thought straight away about Olga's sister, Mila must be a common name. Dave was watching her drive. She crunched the gears occasionally but was a careful driver. She told him they were on a back road and there would be a big house on the right. Tomorrow he would pass the front of this *Dachya* on their way to Georgia where Stalin was born. He should try to see as much as he could about the front of the building. She then took him back to a place near the hotel and dropped him off. She said she would have a nice peaceful evening. The guards were all smiling as he entered the hotel; he knew what was on their minds. It was on his mind and a pity he had no physical contact. So this *Dachya* was the place and from what he could see it was a very large house.

The next day they were off to see Georgian dancers and have a Georgian lunch. On the bus Dave grabbed a window seat on the left. As they left town on the main road he saw that there was a fence around the building and a guard post at the entrance. He tried to take in as much detail as he could; he would have liked the driver to slow down but asking him would be suspicious. In Georgia the dance by men with swords and the food were good. Again he enjoyed the flame- cooked meat even if it was a bit tough. He thought the wine was a bit sweet but tasty. He grabbed a window seat on the right side of the bus. It was becoming dusk as they passed the *Dachya* but he could see the lighting. This place was outside the city limits and seemed to be surrounded by trees. Some of them obscured his vision of the house and the back view with Mila was better. Of course the view of Mila was much better.

Mila joined him in the bar and they left together again. She said she hoped he would come back to finish the job. She was only in prostitution because of this man and she wanted him dead. She said to enjoy the rest of his holiday and would not bother him more. Dave was thinking it was a pity she did not want to bother him more; he was enjoying her company. Now he knew the location but how was he going to get into the compound? That question would have to wait until London.

The next day he walked with Trevor and Olga along the seafront. It was a pebbly beach and not inviting for

Dave. During their walk they were approached by a young man who wanted to buy something. Olga explained that he wanted to buy Dave's shirt, trousers and shoes. He also wanted to buy Trevor's hat. Olga explained even if the shirt and trousers were cheap they had a label and they would fetch a good price on the black market. She was amused and amazed at what they would do with Trevor's hat. Dave was glad to be with Olga, her English was better than the tour guide and she understood English humour. They stopped at a café and Olga did the ordering, Dave was fascinated at the way they were treated, he put it down to having Olga present.

Dave enjoyed the next few days with Olga and Trevor but did not see Mila. One delight was to see Vlada who had come to Sochi to see her sister. Dave told Olga he wanted to buy something to send to Leo. She told him to buy a Union Jack if he could find one. He found one in the market and also an Australian and Canadian flag. He gave them to Vlada and told her he had served with Australians in Japan. Actually Dave could not stop thinking about Leo. That little boy was in his brain.

The flight to Leningrad was delayed and Dave was watching his fellow tourists getting upset. He was sitting back enjoying the chaos. Maybe if he were paying for the trip he might be more upset. On this flight he did not get a window seat but it was very cloudy and so he was not missing much. At the hotel they were met by Mila, Olga's sister, she was telling Dave how much

Leo had enjoyed his presents. He was day dreaming that he had met two Milas and a Vlada and he would marry them all. These ladies were educationally out of his league but he could only dream.

Leningrad was fantastic but these ladies were all he could really see. He definitely had to come back if only to see these sisters and Leo. Actually he was enjoying Russia more than he thought he would and it was not only due to the ladies.

The flight back to London was very smooth and he enjoyed a few beers. The stewardesses were surprised when he asked for Russian beer. Back in London he decided not to move back to Birmingham until his task was completed. He would stick with his present job and await contact with his young lady. Now he just kept daydreaming about Moscow. Every time he went on the underground he was comparing it with the Moscow Metro and London was losing every time.

He visited the park regularly and after a couple of days the young lady sat next to him and said she was Anna. Actually it was Anushka but Anna would do. She hoped Russia had been to his liking and there had been no problems. The holiday could be discussed at a later date but she hoped he enjoyed it. He was listening to everything she said and trying to catch an accent.

"Will you earn five thousand pounds?"

"Yes, but I need much more detail particularly how I will be paid. When am I likely to go back to Russia?

Tell me more about my target. I hope you can answer lots of questions."

"Well there are some unknowns. When we have a date that this man will be in Sochi we will give you two thousand pounds and money for your trip. By the way you did not spend very much of your expenses. Why buy three flags?"

"You must have good spies but the flags were for a young Russian boy, not the normal gift I would give but he appreciated them. I met him in Moscow and bought the flags in Sochi and gave them to his aunt."

Dave was thinking about Leo playing with flags and arranging his coins. It was a very good feeling and the holiday was great.

"If the mission is accomplished you will receive three thousand pounds on your return to England. Normally the target has two weeks or a month at Stalin's *Datchya*, the building you saw. We are not yet sure of his current plans but we will know soon. Sometimes he brings a mistress with him. You must understand these girls or ladies are forced to serve him. Some will have husbands who will be afraid to object. He has a habit of coming on to a balcony late in the evening to enjoy a cigar. During Stalin's time the guards would patrol the perimeter but now they spend most of their time in the evening at the entrance and if they have vodka they will have an early sleep. Last year he spent the month of September at the *Datchya*. We will know his plans soon."

"I am prepared to take on the task and I will stay working in London, I assume I will be going with Intourist and I will tell them I enjoyed the last tour but there was so much I did not see."

"The reports I get are that you are the man for the job."

"Give my regards to Mila."

Anna smiled and said good day as she left.

A week passed and he had his instructions and cash, he looked at the pound notes and most of them were new. He went to Birmingham and gave his sister two hundred pounds and stashed most of the rest in his bedroom. Now he was going to Moscow he had a bit of shopping to do. The group that went to Moscow this time was a similar bunch but no Olga and Trevor. The bus tour was similar but he was looking with more experienced eyes. After the tour he wandered around Red Square and then down by the river. His walk took him into a residential area with a few shops. He had a shopping bag but was not going to buy anything. Finally he found a Metro station, he could read the Cyrillic script as he had spent some spare time studying the alphabet. Within half an hour he was walking to Mila and Vlada's flat: he had memorized the route. Mila answered the door and was shocked to see him standing there.

"I have come to give you some presents and do not need food."

"You are welcome but we have nothing prepared."

"There is no need. Where is Leo? I have a few presents for him."

Leo came from the other room and Dave dipped into his bag and pulled out six Dinky Toy cars and some more coins. Leo's eyes lit up and he gave out a scream. Then Dave presented Mila with chocolates, tinned Cheddar cheese, a bottle of Worcestershire sauce, a jar of marmalade and a bottle of whisky he had bought at duty-free. She made him sit down and have tea and then he said he had a special present for Leo, who was very involved with his cars. He pulled out a purple case and inside was a medal which he explained to Vlada and Mila had been presented to him in Japan by an American general. He wanted Leo to have it. The ladies were in tears and when Leo's mother and aunt told him he flung his arms around Dave and gave him a hug. This was a very emotional evening and Dave went back to his hotel feeling very elated. This little boy was sitting in his head and no other person had ever had this effect on him.

Back at the hotel Dave was thinking this was the best thing he had done in years and maybe it was the best thing he had ever done. It was strange, he was here to kill a man and yet a small boy was more important. The next day Dave wandered around the city and went to look at the university. It sat on a hill and the view across the river was awesome. As he sat there he dreamed about going to this university with Vlada or

Mila. It had magnificent buildings and he would have loved to see inside one.

His walks around Moscow continually took him by Stalin's flats and magnificent old houses and small churches. He was wondering what was there before the flats. He rode the trolley bus and the tram and he found everyone was friendly and helpful. This transport was so cheap. He thought he was seeing more of the city than the average tourist. That night he had a good sleep in the hotel and did not even visit the bar.

At the airport there was the usual palaver with the tour guide continually apologizing for the delay. Dave just sat back and smiled to himself. Obviously the schedule had been set out by someone who had never taken the tour and it would take a bomb to change things. Arriving in Sochi they were transported to the same hotel. After getting to his room he decided to go for a walk. He recognized a couple of the guards and he thought they recognized him. Now he wanted to get a look at the city. The first thing he noticed was that the locals were more reserved than in Moscow. He was a security man used to studying people and his clothes obviously identified him as a foreigner. Again, a couple of young men wanted to buy his clothes but he waved them away. Maybe he should have brought some old clothes with him; that thought made him laugh. The climate was much warmer in Sochi and there were less long overcoats except on a few men he thought might be security. The ladies were dressed in more colourful dresses than in Moscow. Dave was in a very observant mood, watching the cars and police on point duty. Whenever he approached a policeman he always received a broad smile. The pace of life in Sochi was slower than in Moscow and very much slower than London. There seemed to be fewer buildings that took his interest. This place was not like Blackpool or Weston-super-Mare and it did not have the same holiday feel.

After dinner he went to the bar and was greeted by a familiar barman. After a beer he saw Mila. She was in a good mood and they left after a couple of diluted champagnes. They walked for a while and found Mila's car on a quiet side street. Mila drove along the back road explaining that she did not want her car identified driving on the main road with a foreigner. Her information was that the target (no one would name him) was in the *Datchya*. Mila pointed towards the fence and some bushes as they drove past the building. There would be a hole in the fence and a rifle with a silencer placed in the bushes. Mila drove well past the *Datchya* before turning around. He had a final view of the building on the reverse ride. They drove back and he was dropped off near the hotel. Mila would pick him up in two days as the Georgia trip was the next day. She again advised him to see as much as he could as the coach passed the villa. He thought he could be in love with Mila. He walked back to the hotel and had a couple of beers in the bar. As he went to his room he said *spakony notch* to the lady in the booth. She had a big grin and said something back he did not catch.

The pickup by Mila after his trip to Georgia would not be at the hotel but a place near her home, as she did not want to be seen with him that day. It would be near dusk and probably he should have warm clothing. Dave was finding the evenings were warm and realised Mila was acclimatized to Sochi. He would like to see Mila in less clothing but much to his regret that was not going to happen.

The trip to Georgia was uneventful; again there was the same performance and the same food. On the return journey he was able to get a window seat on the bus. He chatted with one or two of his fellow tourists and had a long chat with an American couple. They were complaining that they could not get the food they wanted but were surprised that everyone was smiling. Russians were supposed to be dour people. They liked the Georgian wine which Dave thought sweet; he liked the Georgian beer. The meat on a skewer was good and there was a hot sauce to his liking.

At the hotel he went with the American couple to the bar. They had enjoyed the Georgia trip and Dave had to explain they had crossed a border to get from Russia into Georgia. Then they complained that they did not have a stamp in their passports. They were from the Midwest; a small town in Iowa called Grinnell. They were farmers and a good crop had allowed them a holiday. They had come to England and found this cheap trip to Russia. There was going to be plenty to tell their friends and relatives. Dave introduced the lady to a semi-sweet Georgian wine and she loved it. She wanted her husband to buy a case. Dave told him to talk to the tour guide as he thought it was possible to get some shipped to the States. He received a card from the man but excused himself for not having a business card; he was not too keen on revealing his address. He left them in the bar and greeted the lady in the cubicle. She enquired if he had a lady friend but he apologized and said no. He wished Mila was with him but he had to concentrate on the job at hand.

The next day he spent walking around the city and sitting near the so-called beach. He also wandered around the market where he saw a lot of military medals and clothing. There were one or two interesting knives on sale but he decided to buy only a pen knife. What could he buy for his sister? She did not know he was in Russia and she had not known about his first trip. He decided to buy *Matryoshka* dolls, which he could always say he picked them from any airport. Back at the hotel he changed into some old clothes and had a jacket although it was still warm. He remembered to put gloves in the inside pockets of the jacket and was now ready for his night's work.

He walked out to the designated spot and waited to be picked up by Mila. As he entered the car he smelt her perfume, he liked the smell.

"What is that perfume? I would like to buy a bottle for my sister."

"The hotel has a shop selling this perfume, ask for Ocean for ladies and they will be glad to sell you a bottle."

Mila was shaking her head. Here was a man going to kill someone and he is asking about perfume. The perfume was not for his girlfriend but his sister. What a man!

They reached a spot where the back of the *Datchya* could be seen. Mila reminded Dave of the bushes and to be careful as he ran across open ground. It was dusk but still light enough to see a figure passing across it.

"Don't worry, I do not want to be caught but if there is any problem you disappear."

Dave left the car and ran crouched across the open ground to a clump of trees. He stopped and listened, there was no sound but he waited till he had his breath. He then crept on all fours to the bushes. As he lay he saw the rifle and ammunition, it was not well hidden. Someone must have left it the previous night. That was a good sign as no one was patrolling the fence. This was a very good rifle with a silencer and a night scope. He took a very good look at it and could see no maker's mark or a serial number. The rifle felt very easy in his hands and had a feel he enjoyed. He wondered whether this rifle had been made from different parts. There was no way of testing it so he had to rely on it being accurate and as good as it looked. While he was loading the rifle he heard a sound. He froze and listened intently, his heart was racing. Then it happened again. It was an owl. Dave lay flat and relaxed after all he was in the country. He looked around and it was getting darker so he decided to move to the fence. A neat hole had been cut and all he had to do was fold the fence away so there was plenty of room to crawl through. He had to be careful his clothes did not get caught on the cut fence. He reminded himself to be careful on the way back.

He entered the perimeter and slowly crawled along a hedgerow. This area of the garden was not well lit. He was behind the hedge but had a perfect view of the villa (he thought of it as a villa). Crawling along behind the hedge he found a spot where there was a perfect view of the balcony; it was well lit so he might not need the scope. He lay flat and listened to the sounds. All he could hear was the chatter of the guards at the front gate. It would be good if they had plenty of vodka to spend the night. As he lay there he was trying to make sure he did not fall asleep. Mila thought that it might be cold but Dave thought it was quite warm.

At about nine p.m. a balding, well-built man came onto the balcony. He stretched his arms and took a deep breath; he was alone. Then he pulled out a cigar and was about to light it when a bullet pierced his skull just below his right ear. He fell to the floor of the balcony without a sound. The rifle had made a ffuuutt! sound that could hardly have been heard. The guards at the entrance did not hear it, they were babbling on uninterrupted. Dave relaxed for a minute and then slowly retreated to the fence and carefully exited through the hole. Putting back the fence made him stop and think if he had missed anything. Now he had to dispose of the rifle, he could not take it back to Mila's car. He had used gloves so there were no fingerprints but to throw away a rifle of this quality was not something he wanted to do.

On his way to the fence, he had seen a depression with some bushes near the end of it. He thought they would use dogs to trace his escape so he decided to throw the rifle under the bushes and keeping going along the track. He ran along the road and darted into the long grass on the side and doubled back and forth along the side. Mila was watching and wondered what he was doing. When he found the car, Mila was patiently waiting and very ready to leave.

"The job has been done and I hope you will now have a better life."

Mila did not reply but he saw tears running down her cheek.

"All that running around in the grass was to confuse the dogs they will surely use. I must say if situations were different, I would propose marriage."

Mila could not believe what she was hearing. This was a man like no other. He had just killed a man and was thinking about marriage. The rest of the drive was in silence. She dropped him off near the hotel and told him they would not meet again but she thanked him.

Suddenly Dave felt quite emotional he was not going to see Mila again, he thought it was a great loss. After a short walk Dave went to the hotel and straight to the bar. He met the American couple who asked about his evening. Dave was tempted to tell them about mission accomplished but decided to tell them that the market was cheap but they had to haggle. They did not understand the word haggle so he searched his brain and found barter. The next day was a free day so he found the shop selling perfumes. The sellers were surprised he wanted a Russian perfume called Ocean, they expected he would want a French perfume such as Chanel. He also bought some after shave called Ocean which had a similar smell and would remind him of Mila.

The next morning the flight to Leningrad was of course delayed and while most of his fellow tourists complained Dave sat back and enjoyed the mayhem. The Americans said this could not happen in America. They were going back to London and then home via New York and then to Des Moines.

After landing in Leningrad and a ride to the hotel he left the hotel and wandered about the city. The tour to the museum was very brief and he told himself he would come back one day and spend at least one day in this fantastic place. On the way to the airport the American was excitedly telling him he had ordered a case of wine to be shipped to his home. Dave reminded him to pick up his duty-free at Moscow airport as it was much cheaper than at Heathrow. Before he left he thanked his guide and said that during his second trip he saw and did much more than the first. She was not to know that he had exterminated a Russian pest.

On the way home from Gatwick Dave was thinking he would love to see more of Russia but that might be too difficult and dangerous. He was now waiting for his reward but Mila's tears could be reward enough. Dave had never proposed marriage before even though it was half-heartedly. He realised he was in love with at least three Russian women. Looking around on his trip to Birmingham he could see no woman coming close to his Russian ladies. His sister loved the *Matryoshkas* and the perfume. She was asking when he would come back to Birmingham but she did not ask where he bought her gifts. He told her he had some things to do in London but he would definitely come back to Birmingham. The perfume on his sister reminded him of Mila.

He sat on the park bench and a young lady sat beside him and introduced herself as Anna. He was a bit confused but welcomed her. She told him her real name was Anna (she had told him that before but maybe he had thought that an alias) and Dave had made her very happy. He was hoping he had made several Russian ladies happy; there were two Milas, one Vlada and now an Anna. He looked at her and winked hoping she would be confused but that did not stop her.

"You have made hundreds of Russians happy, in fact maybe a thousand and here is the rest of your reward. I think they received happiness cheaply. I am so proud of you."

"Now can you do something for me? Is it possible to get me a clean rifle with a silencer? By clean I mean not having previously been used. Of course I will pay, I hope it is as good as the one I used in Sochi that was an excellent rifle and I assume it was Russian."

"That is a tall order but leave it with me and I will see you here in three days. Yes, it was a Russian rifle."

With that Anna walked off and Dave sat back thinking of the last two weeks. He would love to be in Russia chatting with his lady friends. There was a big smile on his face as he went back to his flat. He dressed for his work; his night duty was a happy one. Oh for a flight on Aeroflot and travel on the Metro. He daydreamed all night about Moscow and Sochi.

Three days later he was sitting on the bench again when Anna joined him. She sat very close and he was tempted to put his arm around her.

"What you want will cost two hundred and fifty pounds and will take a while to get. Do you still want it?"

"Yes, I will pay and I hope it is as good as the one I used in Sochi. By the way have you any news?"

"No news yet except that you succeeded. Your request will take time but you have to be patient. As for this new rifle someone will deliver it to your flat and you will pay him cash. We of course have your address but there is no need to tell me unless you wish to."

As she left he felt that he always had a good feeling when she was around. Now he started to think about that last remark but he had missed the chance. He had forgotten to smell her perfume but he would recommend Ocean. As she walked away he loved the sway of her hips. Again he had a pleasant night duty, 'daydreaming' most of the time.

Dave relaxed into his normal routine. He would finish night duty and pick up a newspaper at the newsagent. The newsagent would tell him all the local news. He would sleep in the morning and relax in the afternoon. One afternoon he was listening to the radio when there was a knock at the door. It was Boris.

"Come in and would you like a cup of tea?"

"Yes, thank you, no milk, no sugar It is also quite .Russian to offer a visitor a drink but not necessarily tea."

"I am sorry. I don't keep vodka or any other spirits in my home; I see by that in the holdall you have my present. I hope it is a good one the other was so good I had trouble throwing it away. I checked it out and was worried I might need two bullets but it was perfect."
"Yes, this present is a good one and will cost you two hundred and fifty pounds. You did a good job in Sochi; you literally blew his brains out. His body was not found till the next morning by a cleaner. The local police, the military and the KGB were all there within the day. They soon found the hole in the fence and they had dogs trace your escape route. Obviously you did a bit of

circling and back tracking at the end before you got in Mila's car. The dogs and handlers became confused. The interesting thing was that they did not find the rifle. We had an operative waiting to pick it up when the searching died down but we were beaten to it. For some reason a local criminal, a drug-dealer was in the area and he found the gun and took it back to his flat. We are wondering whether he had a stash of drugs nearby, it seemed a strange place for him to be. Unfortunately for him his flat was raided; the police were looking for drugs which they found along with the rifle. They charged him with murder and drug possession. Of course he pleaded innocent and showed them where he found the gun. They could not admit missing it so he is in prison awaiting trial."

"Well, two birds with one shot. I hate drug pushers and one or two less is to my liking. I have always wanted to remove some from society."

After a long chat Boris left with a shaking of hands and two hundred and fifty pounds. Dave put on gloves and assembled the rifle. It was brand new, had never been fired and had no markings; it had probably been stolen in pieces from the manufacturer. Dave liked the feel of this gun. He had another happy night shift and informed his employer he would take a few days off. The next night he watched a fancy car drive up and park under his back window. He nipped out onto his balcony and stood behind a pillar. It was well after dusk and quite dark but as a man crossed the courtyard he was hit in the neck by a bullet. The man went down without a cry. This was a courtyard surrounded on all sides by flats and no one was about in the evening. They were all probably having tea or listening to the radio.

Dave went back into his flat and disassembled the rifle and put it in a suitcase. He locked the case and left the flat by the back door. He caught the bus to Paddington station and then a train to Birmingham. While waiting for the bus he did not hear any police sirens probably meaning the man had not been found. The man he had just killed was a drug dealer who Dave had identified in the night club as well as other places. This man was putting other people in misery and Dave put him out of his misery. Dave had no problem in killing a drug dealer and shooting him was easier than strangling him.

The buses and trains were on time and he had a chance to get a beer in the station. He arrived in Birmingham late in the evening and took the bus to his home. He used his key to enter and found his sister getting ready for bed. They kissed and he gave her a month's rent. She gave him two letters, one was from Trevor and Olga. It was full of praise for Dave's second visit and he was Leo's hero. Leo now wanted to learn English and one day meet Dave again. This gave Dave a very good feeling. The second letter was from Cyprus offering Dave a job. Fred had set up a security business and it was going very well and Fred needed help he could trust. This was the news Dave had been waiting for and now he could settle his affairs in England. He had to make sure his sister was taken care of and his mother's grave was regularly cleaned. He would contact his aunty (his mother's sister) and give her money for flowers. He would send a letter to Trevor and Olga giving his possible address in Cyprus. They had made quite an impression on Dave.

The next day he put the silencer in the holdall with the ammunition and some other rifle parts. He then went for a walk along the canal in Winson Green. This was a very familiar canal that still had plenty of barges. As a young man he had walked along the canal towpath regularly and he knew the location of the drop. He checked there were no barges about and when he reached a railway bridge he dropped the gun parts into the water. It was very murky with a film of oil on the surface. Dave thought that they would not drain it as it was used all the time by barges. He then had a pleasant walk along the canal and did not meet another soul. He was very familiar with this canal and as a young boy he had seen many barges passing along many pulled by horses. He came up from the towpath and found a pub where he had a beer. He much preferred the German or Russian beer.

The next day he put the barrel and other parts except the wooden stock in the holdall. He caught a Midland Red bus to Smethwick and walked along the canal to near the Galton Bridge. It was another canal walk he knew well. It brought back memories when he was young. He found a secluded spot and dropped the barrel and other parts in the water; now he had to get rid of the stock. He found a pub near the bridge and had a pint of beer. Again he was thinking he much preferred the Russian beer, English beer was warm and he was now accustomed to colder beer.

It was approaching Bonfire Night (November 5th) so he walked around the area and found a large bonfire in preparation. The children had made a good job of collecting firewood. The fire was on an old bomb site and there was quite a space for a large bonfire. The next day after it became dark he walked to the bonfire and found it well alight. The children and adults were watching the fireworks so he walked around the back of the fire and threw the stock into it. His aim was good and it went well into the fire. He then joined the others watching the fireworks. He walked home with a good feeling, Mila's tears were still in his memory. The next day he checked the still burning embers and could see no sign of the stock. Everything so far was going to plan and Dave could relax.

He took the train back to London. He was in London in his flat listening to the music on the radio when there was a knock on the door. He opened it to be greeted by a policeman.

"Good afternoon, sir, we are looking for anyone who may have seen what happened a few nights ago. We have been here a few times but no one was in and I would like to ask a few questions."

"What happened? I have just come back from Birmingham this afternoon. I have spent a few days there with my sister. Anyway what happened?"

"Did you ever see a fancy car parked outside your window?"

"I work nights and have no car of my own but some mornings I did see an expensive car in the car park."

The PC said, "The man who was shot in the courtyard was a drug dealer and he would visit his girlfriend who lives in the opposite block to you. His car was full of drugs and just the other day the drug squad took it away. It was parked outside your window. From your balcony you would have had a perfect view of the shooting."

"I am sorry, constable I was not here. I will have to go to the shops to get the latest gossip. The newsagent will tell me everything."

"Thank you for your time, sir, we think it was a gangland killing."

Dave went to the shops and received some gory details. The shopkeeper said he had not seen Dave for a while and Dave told him he had been in Birmingham. The shopkeeper was not too unhappy with someone getting rid of a piece of excrement. Dave expressed surprise that it had happened right under his balcony and he was not there. The newsagent said he had many happy customers and everyone was praising the person who got rid of this piece of shit.

Dave gave in his notice at work and with the landlord. This was a council flat but the landlord lived with his lady friend and rented it out. He was glad to get his flat back. Dave packed his belongings, said goodbye to the flat and went to Birmingham. Now he was going to start a new life. He thought maybe in Sochi; Mila would also have a new life. It was a cold damp day in Birmingham and he was looking forward to Cyprus.

In Birmingham he informed his sister he had a job in Cyprus and he would try to send her rent money if he could. He told her she should find a man. She winked as she told him that might be a possibility. He then thought he should find a woman. He was still a bachelor and had not even had a steady girlfriend.

The flight to Cyprus was pleasant and he had a window seat. He could see a lot of the Mediterranean as there were only a few clouds. Fred met him at Nicosia airport and was talking ten to the dozen. Dave told him to slow down and they could talk over a beer. Fred said he now preferred the wine but agreed a quiet chat was a good idea. Fred now ran a security company protecting large houses owned by expatriates. He employed Greeks, Turks, Yugoslavs and one young Brit who would be called up soon. Fred had some proposals of work in Africa and wanted Dave to take over the Cypriot company. He wanted Dave to be a partner so that when all the formalities had been fixed Fred could go off to Africa with peace of mind.

Dave said, "Let me look over your company and if I take the job we will need to find more customers."

"I like the way you think, look all you want."

Fred gave Dave open access to the accounts and Dave also met the workforce. Dave was never going to turn down the job; he saw there was plenty of money to be made in this company. Cyprus also reminded him in some ways of Sochi; of course he was here to protect people, not kill them. Fred said the real big money was in Africa and he was keen to get there as soon as possible. Dave looked at the large houses that did not seem to have security and in the next week he talked two owners into signing up for night security. There was a house with a high wall so he thought he would give it a try. He rang the bell on the gate and a familiar figure opened the gate.

"Hello, Boris. I came to talk to the owner about security but I think he does not need it."

"I am the owner and I don't need security but I am glad to see you. Fred had told me you were coming. Anna will be happy to see you. I hope that the rifle was useful."

"Yes, it was used and disposed of. Does Anna know the details?"

"No, only I know and I approve. Anna will be here in a few days and I am encouraging her to come and live in Cyprus. I am sorry to rush this conversation but I am awaiting an important international phone call. I will see you in the near future."

Dave wondered what kind of business Boris was in to own such a nice house. He guessed he knew Fred through the London security companies. He mentioned to Fred that he had met Boris and Fred told him to stay friendly with him. Fred did not know of Dave and Boris's relationship. Dave was really intrigued by Boris but maybe he was in a bigger league.

Fred left for Africa and Dave was in charge and he felt this was going to be a lifetime job. He made friends with the workforce and listened to their stories. He started to understand the politics of Cyprus from both the Greek and Turkish side. Now he had to make himself aware of what was going on in Cyprus so he could plan for the future. He took a drive around the island and saw lots of beautiful homes which were all potential business. He also saw poorer areas where there was potential to find thieves.

One day he was sitting at his desk when in walked Anna. He looked up and she smiled.

"That big desk suits you, but I prefer you on a bench. I cannot get my mind off you and when I found out you were in Cyprus I decided to come to live with you."

Dave was shocked and all he could say was "what about the age difference? I am probably ten years older than you? You don't really know me I could be a killer."

Anna said, "The age difference does not matter to me. You are the man I want. Killing for a good reason is no crime in my book. I assume you might like me and want to live with me."

"We hardly know each other. Maybe we should have a trial period, I have been a bachelor for a long time. I know I like you and would want to live with you"

"Yes, a trial period sounds good. Now will you take me to dinner?"

"Yes, of course but I need to close the office."

"No problem. I will go and collect some clothes and tell Uncle Boris I will not be back for a few days,"

"So he is your uncle. I thought he could be."

Anna left the office and Dave sat thinking about his good luck and also how sure Anna was about the future. He sat contemplating the relationship of Anna and Boris. Maybe Boris was Anna's father's brother and wanted revenge. This was not the time to ask but it was a question for the future.

Dave picked a quiet restaurant with cubicles. He did not know where the conversation would go and did not want strangers listening. Anna arrived and they deposited her clothes in his flat. There was not much furniture as he had not looked at was available. Anna smiled and said, "We, I mean I, will have to furnish this flat."

Dave didn't care. All he could see was a lovely figure he had never really noticed before; she was so feminine. She was one of his Russian ladies and she was going to live with him.

At the restaurant Anna started telling her story. After her mother died she was taken in by her mother's brother Boris. (Dave had got the relationship wrong). They lived in Russia for a couple of years and then Boris was transferred to Hungary. She was young but she liked Hungary it was a little freer than Russia. They were in Hungary for a while and then in 1956 there was an uprising and they took the opportunity to escape to the West. There was only a short time to get out. Boris had a job in the British controlled part of Germany and then transferred to England. (They could have been in Germany at the same time). Boris had a good job and they prospered and made friends with other Russians even some White Russians. She went to school and quickly learnt English, she was planning to go to university but got a good job in an office. She wanted to take some time out but her uncle moved to Cyprus and asked her to join him and his wife.

"Then I learnt you were here and there was no stopping me. I have to go back for a few days to clear up a few things but I am coming back to live with you."

"Well, I suppose that is settled as long as the trial period works."

"It will work. The news from Sochi is that Mila has given up the 'game' and is soon to get married. She says you are the nicest man she had ever met. What did you think of Russia?"

"I liked what I saw and met interesting people. Four days in Moscow and Leningrad were not enough but a few days in Sochi were enough. I loved the metro in Moscow and the museum in Leningrad was just fabulous.

"I would love to spend more time there.

"I was lucky on my first trip to meet a Russian lady and her English husband. Through them I met her sisters and nephew. These were educated ladies and I fell in love with the son Leo. I gave him some coins and the pleasure on his face has stuck with me ever since. On my second trip I gave him some Dinky Toys and a medal I received in Japan. Apparently he wants to learn English and visit me sometime. I will give his aunt my address."

Anna rushed around the table and gave Dave a big kiss.

"You have just proved the kind of man you are and you are mine so let's go to your flat and try your bed."

Singapore Charley

"Welcome again to Singapore, meet my wife Nur."

"Thanks, Charley. Meet my wife Li."

Charley and Trevor were meeting again in Singapore after many years. They had been in the army and their last posting together was in Singapore. Trevor had been transferred to Hong Kong while Charley stayed in Singapore.

Charley said, "This is my father-in-law's car. I only have a small one not big enough for four people and luggage. It should not take long to get to our place as long as there is no traffic jam caused by an accident. Often cyclists get hit or a cart turns over but I guess it is the same in Hong Kong."

Trevor was sitting in the passenger seat looking everywhere "I have not driven for a while and the traffic here seems to be more than I remember but not as bad as Hong Kong. Kowloon where we lived is a traffic-jam place."

"Yes, Singapore is growing fast and we are starting to get traffic jams. I know most of the back roads but even they are getting congested. I thought about getting a cycle like almost everyone else but I have not ridden since I was a kid."

"I've never considered a bike. Our wives in the back seem to be getting on well using a mixture of Cantonese and English so I can understand everything. I am smiling at their banter. I understand my Cantonese could be useful in Singapore but I suppose I will always be speaking English."

Charley said, "I can only speak English and that is Brummie English. The locals enjoy my English, they always thought that the English language was spoken in the same way. I tell them the English they hear in the posh hotels is upper class English and people like me speak with an accent depending on where we come from in England. That always seems to amuse them. We are getting more tourists now but I have yet to come across a Brummie, although they might not admit to their origins."

"Why not try to learn a local language?"

"I have no time and although my father-in-law is a nice bloke he works me hard. Everyone including Nur wants me to speak English, she is preparing for when we can afford to go to England. I do know some unsavoury words and greetings but I don't tend to use them often. I tell the locals in the market if they come across tourists with my accent to give them bargains. One day the market people identified a couple with funny accents but when I met them they were from the North of England. I was originally from Manchester and it was good to hear their accent. One good thing about Singapore is that I am almost average height and could get lost in a crowd. Not many people look down on me here; I love the feeling of being average height. Everywhere I have been I am always the smallest."

They both laughed at that comment.

Charley was born in Manchester and moved to Birmingham when he was five-years-old. He had been a small baby and was always small for his age; he was initially picked on at school. After acquiring the local accent children were still cruel about his size. His mother kept telling him he would grow tall soon but soon never came. The reason they came to Birmingham was that his maternal grandparents lived there. His grandfather was an experienced tool maker and had lived in Birmingham many years. He worked in the Jewellery Quarter and had found Charley's dad a job in the same area. They lived two streets from where Charley lived and as his grandmother did not work he would often go to her after school. She would give him tea and homemade cake which he loved. When the weather was fine particularly in the summer Charley would play with the other children in the street.

At home the family always had a problem. Even though his mom worked they seemed to be continually broke and Charley's grandparents bought most of his clothes. Charley did not know that his father was a gambler. In the evening his parents would always argue and although Charley did not listen, he realised it was always about money. He would often spend overnight at his grandparents' house and the best benefit was the breakfast. At home his mom would put him to bed before the arguments started; she was protecting Charley from potential abuse. At his grandparents' house he could stay up later and breakfast was often bacon and egg with toast.

School became easier by an unusual route. He started playing marbles with an older boy and they became friends. He often let the older boy win to keep him happy. The older boy became his protector although he still had to learn to take care of himself. Life in the street became easier but it was different at home. One morning Charley's mother gave him his breakfast and he noticed a black mark on her left cheek. It looked like a bruise but he was not sure so he said nothing. He went to school and at tea he mentioned to his grandmother about the mark. His granddad overheard and went storming out of the house.

"Stop, Bill! It may be nothing, don't do anything rash."

Later his grandfather came home and told his wife that Charley was going to stay with them permanently. She should collect his clothes the next morning. He told Charley's parents to sort out their problems without Charley around; he was angry and said he wanted to kill Charley's father. Charley pleaded with him to leave his father alone and his grandmother berated his grandfather. Charley was put to bed with his grandmother giving him a big kiss.

After a few weeks Charley's mother (Jill) visited to say that two large men were looking for her husband who owed a lot of money. These were gambling debts. The next day Jill reported that her husband had left a note to say he had to disappear as he owed too much money. Her mother begged her to live with them and forget her husband. Jill moved in with her parents to share a bedroom with Charley. Charley was not sure what was happening but was happy his mother was coming to live with them. He loved this time; he would get plenty of kisses and was tucked up in bed every night. As he grew up he was still small but he was loved; he had plenty to eat but was not growing. He always hated being the smallest in his class. Even when he left infants' school to go to junior school he was smaller than most of the children still in the infants.

Living with his grandparents had some advantages. His grandfather taught him to play games such as chess, draughts and dominoes. This was useful on cold winter nights. His grandmother let him help her make cakes and he loved to lick the bowls after the dough was put in the oven. Roast potatoes were his favourite but cabbage was not on his preferred list. Occasionally the four sat down to play card games; this was a happy household.

Charley loved Friday evenings. It was when he had his bath in the living room near the fire. His mother would put him to bed and then go downstairs to have her bath in the tin bath. His grandfather and grandmother had their baths on a Saturday. As he grew older he was aware that ladies' bodies were different and needed to be hidden from young boys. He was upset when boys in the street started to talk about female bodies. He worshipped his mother and grandmother. The problem with growing up was that he had to sleep in the downstairs front room so his mother could keep the bedroom and his bath time was disrupted.

Charley was approaching fifteen and was about to leave school; he had to find a job. His grandfather did work for a jeweller who had a young man who was about to be conscripted. This man did odd jobs around the workshop including sweeping the floorboards. Charley was hired to sweep up and help any of the jewellers who needed it. It was impressed on him that his sweepings would go into a bag which would be incinerated later. At some stage the floor boards would be replaced and incinerated. This was done to catch all gold filings produced when the jewellers were working the gold mainly to make rings and necklaces.

Charley loved his job and even sweeping the floor had a purpose. Going to work every day was a pleasure and at weekends he was often bored. He was too small to play football or cricket. He learned how the jewellers were manipulating gold and he would often be giving them tools when they were doing intricate work. The jewellers taught him how to identify gem stones. Most of the stones were diamonds or zircons but there were many other stones; deep red rubies were his favourite. All the jewellers were helpful and showed him how to view stones through a magnifying glass. He loved to view diamonds and look at the imperfections and the cuts. He learned about gold and the settings the jewellers were using and sweeping up had him thinking about the losses of gold when the jewellers were making rings or necklaces. Charley's boss was very happy with him as he was always happy and smiling. Charley always liked to go to work and was unhappy when he was sick.

One day his boss asked him if he would like to see some diamonds; Charley could be his bodyguard. Of course Charley was happy to go and wondered where they were going. His big surprise was that it was a pub at the end of the street. They did not leave the Jewellery Quarter and Charley passed this pub every day. Charley was under age and could only drink pop. He sat with his boss at a table wondering what would happen next. An old man with a long beard approached their table; he had a skull cap so Charley knew he was a Jew. His boss greeted this man and introduced Charley. The man did not speak and sat at the table, he then pulled out a purple pouch and a small rectangular box. He poured diamonds from the pouch into the box. These diamonds were sparkling in the light and Charley was mesmerized. Charley's boss looked at a few diamonds and gave his magnifying glass to Charley. The Jewish man took an interest.

"What do you see?"

"These are nicely cut diamonds if a little bit small. One diamond seems to have a flaw or maybe an inclusion. I think I might need a glass with a bigger magnification. Do you have any uncut diamonds?"

"I like this boy. He asks good questions and says good things. I do have two uncut diamonds which I keep in my pocket; they are like a lucky charm. You may see them and tell me how I should cut them. Just one minute I have them inside a pocket inside a pocket."

Charley was enjoying this talk better than his pop.

"Well, these are rather large stones but too many cuts will reduce them too much. I suggest minimal cutting to produce large stones that might need further work. I am not an expert at cutting but try to keep these as large as possible. Will you cut them yourself?"

"In my workshop I have many diamond cutters but I regularly cut stones; these I will keep in their raw state for a while. I love this boy he must come and visit my workshop one day. By the way, you are Charley and I am Jacob. It has been my pleasure to meet you."

Charley's boss bought some stones after a bit of haggling. They all shook hands as they left the pub. Charley's boss was very happy and told Charley he had made a good impression. "I see that Jacob likes you and he is an expert diamond cutter. He comes here regularly to sell diamonds and only seems to want to come to this pub. I am glad you made a good impression and when he comes next time you will come too."

At home Charley was telling his grandfather about his day. His grandfather was smiling all the time, he knew the pub and knew there were plenty of transactions going on during the day but not at night.

"I wondered if this little old man could get robbed."

"This happens all the time in the Jewellery Quarter and he will have some muscle you did not see. It is possible the publican has some deal with Jacob. These people work on trust and a handshake is all that is needed."

Charley met Jacob several times and it was a pleasure and a learning experience each time. One time Charley asked Jacob what he did with his best stones. Jacob smiled the first one Charley had seen. Jacob told him his best stones remained in his workshop and buyers had to visit him. He was comfortable with lesser stones but the very best stones were expensive. Jacob then invited Charley to visit his workshop where he could see everything including the best stones. Charley asked where it was in Amsterdam and to his surprise was told it was in Antwerp. Charley had no idea where Antwerp was. In fact he hardly knew the location of Amsterdam and so he had to go to the library to look up Antwerp. He was keen to get a passport and his grandfather was helping him all the way. Bill was very proud of his grandson making friends with a Jewish diamond dealer; it could only be a good thing. Charley's boss was also pleased with him as he had made friends with Jacob and that was not an easy task. Some of the other jewellers were telling Charley to learn as much as he could and they would expect a report on his return. They wanted to know about every detail of Jacob's work.

Charley received his passport and his boss said he would finance his trip. He had never been outside Birmingham except when he came from Manchester when he was young. His grandmother took him to the bus depot in Digbeth where he bought a ticket. The driver informed him that this was a coach not a bus. Charley thought it looked like a single decker bus but the seats were more comfortable than on the local buses. The coach would take him to London where he would catch a coach to Dover. Charley was enjoying all the scenery and that kept him awake; he thought he could sleep in the seat. First he saw other parts of Birmingham but what impressed him most was Oxford. The old buildings were beautiful and he did not realize they were part of the university. The bus station in London impressed him too; there were so many buses from all parts of England. He found the next coach that was waiting so he had no time to leave the garage. He only saw a bit of London from the coach but he was more interested in the countryside rather than the town. Dover was interesting as he had never seen the sea. The bus station was close to the docks and he could smell the sea. There were many sea gulls and Charley stood on the dock watching them and the fishermen. The port was full of ships and he had some time before catching the ferry. He wandered along the dock and watched some fishing trawlers unloading their catches. This was all new to Charley and he was enjoying the experience.

The ferry was crossing overnight to Ostende and would arrive early in the morning. Charley did not have a berth and was told to sleep on a bench in the bar. He couldn't sleep so he spent most of the night on the deck. This was all new experience and he spent most of the time watching lights from land and other boats.

He had been told not to use his schoolboy French as where he was going they spoke Flemish and preferred to be spoken to in English. Arriving in Belgium he was directed to the bus station and the ticket purchase kiosk. He paid for Antwerp with two pound notes. He put the Belgian change in his left pocket. Again the scenery was different. Alighting in Antwerp he showed a man the address and was directed in perfect English. So far he had only said Antwerp twice and thank you twice. On the street he saw men in fur hats; he thought they must be Jews. The building he entered looked a bit seedy but inside it was very clean. As soon as he asked for Jacob everyone was smiling. It looked like they were expecting him and several shook his hand.

Jacob's workshop was quite large and Charley was greeted by Jacob with a big hug and a kiss on both cheeks. Jacob introduced his second son who was not much older than Charley. Jacob told him to come to the office as he could see the workshop later. In the office Jacob produced his best stones and Charley had to admire them. He was allowed to examine each one. Then Jacob produced a large stone which Charley examined.

He said, "This is a large stone but I don't like the cut. I think you should sell it to someone who does not understand diamonds."

Charley thought Jacob would have a heart attack he was laughing so much; he nearly fell off his chair.

His son looked concerned and was holding his father. Jacob controlled himself and said, "You say things I cannot expect. This is one of the uncut diamonds I keep in my pocket and I decided that as you were coming I would give it a rough cut. I think I could sell it at a profit without any more work but I will work on it till I am satisfied."

"As I cannot afford it, I suggest you do a better job," said Charley.

Again, Jacob was laughing loudly and it prompted a few of the workers to enter the office.

"No one talks to me like you and this diamond will enter my pocket until I think of you."

Jacob's son took Charley aside and told him his father rarely smiled and he was making him laugh like he had never heard before. Charley was invited to dinner after he had been escorted to his hotel. Jacob insisted he pay the bill for two nights. Charley had a room with a bed and a wash stand. It was fairly bare. The toilet was down the hall. The lady on the desk spoke English and asked him where he was from and how did he know Jacob. He told her he worked in a jeweller's workshop and they bought diamonds from Jacob. Charley started to think he had said too much but he could not retract it.

He was picked up by Jacob's son and taken to dinner. Charley had never been in a Jewish house before but he noticed all the women including girls were dressed in black and had their heads covered. All the men except the young boys had beards. The walls were bare; there were no pictures or paintings. Everyone shook his hand except the young girls and the children. All he could say was thank you which he did several times. He was ushered to the chair on the right hand of Jacob who was at the end of the table. On Jacob's left hand side was his wife. This was a large long table. When everyone was seated Jacob rose and gave a speech in a language Charley could not understand. Then Jacob spoke in English and introduced his adopted son Charley.

Charley was taken aback and did not know what to say. Jacob's son whispered that he should just nod and enjoy the food. He certainly enjoyed the chicken but was not too keen on something called gefilte fish. After the dinner Jacob's wife praised Charley for making her husband laugh, it was apparently a rare occasion. She said her son was so astonished he could not remember his father laughing like that before. There was a lot of talk in a language he did not understand but everyone spoke to him in English. He drank water and a peculiar brown liquid that tasted a bit like weak beer. At the end of the evening Charley was escorted by Jacob's son to the hotel. He found he was very tired and had a good night's sleep. In the morning he had what was called a continental breakfast. He still chose egg and bacon but also enjoyed pancakes with honey. At the end of the meal he thought he had eaten too much.

Charley spent the day in the workshop watching the workers cutting stones, mainly diamonds. He was given some lunch which consisted of black bread, a piece of cheese, a slice of meat and some kind of sauce. He enjoyed it and ate it all; that pleased Jacob. Jacob and his son took him to the bus station to catch the bus to Ostende. He was hugged and kissed on both cheeks; all the women were absent.

The ferry was again overnight to Dover but this time the crossing was smooth and he found a comfortable chair. He slept for a few hours. . In Dover he had to buy a ticket to Birmingham via London. He must have slept because the bus was pulling into the London bus station as he awoke. Again he did not see much of London. He even slept on the coach to Birmingham; the seats were so comfortable for a little lad.

Back home he had many stories for his family and his workmates. His grandfather was especially pleased he had been to Belgium as that was where his father had been killed in World War One. He was asking about cutting diamonds. His grandmother and mother were most interested in the Jewish household. They asked what the ladies were wearing. He had to describe all the food and other things he had seen in Belgium; neither his mother nor his grandparents had been on the continent.

Charley was wondering whether he could cut diamonds. He now knew how but he thought he might be afraid of spoiling a good stone. All the jewellers were interested when he told them about Jacob's workshop and how the men were cutting diamonds.

Charley joined the workshop when he was fifteen and all the jewellers told him he would grow taller one day but his growth was slow. Actually the jewellers enjoyed having this happy little lad about their work. Time passed quickly and then Charley was conscripted when he was eighteen. His boss said he would have a job after his army service. Jill was very upset and hoped they would reject him due to his height; his grandfather thought that a possibility. No one in the army seemed to care about his height and he was told to report at Snow Hill station. He was pleased.

Charley's father had disappeared and so only his mother and grandparents were at the station to give him a tearful farewell. This was going to be a new phase of his life.

He met his fellow conscripts at Snow Hill Station. He was definitely the smallest, there were several six footers. Several fellows asked him why he did not get a deferment and he told them he was told he would grow a few inches in the army. They all had a good laugh and Charley was thinking his best strategy was to keep them laughing. In fact they were a nice bunch of fellows and none of them wanted to join the army and no one bullied him.

They arrived at Aldershot training camp and were lined up by a corporal who told them they would get their kit and be assigned to a billet. As he walked along the line, the corporal spied Charley.

"Well, soldier, you are going to be a challenge. I don't think we will have a uniform to fit you."

"Well, if you let me go I will come back in a year when I have grown a few inches."

The whole troop started laughing but the corporal ordered them to be quiet. He looked at Charley, shook his head and walked to the end of the line. He led them into a tent where they would collect their kit. The sergeant giving out the kit, took one look at Charley, shook his head and ordered the smallest uniform they had. The whole uniform was too big. The trousers were too long, the sleeves were too long. The collar was too big and the waist was too large. At least he had boots that fitted if slightly too large but they gave him some thick socks. Charley was wondering how he could make this uniform fit. If this was the smallest they had he had to be the smallest man in the army.

The parade sergeant took one look at Charley and said, "You are in luck, son, one of our conscripts was training to be a tailor. You are both excused until you look presentable."

Charley met Arthur from the south of London who was training to be a tailor. They immediately enjoyed each other's company and Arthur could easily rectify most of the problems except the collar size. When next on parade, the sergeant pulled at Charley's uniform and seemed satisfied. They were then marching for what Charley thought was hours. He could just about keep up but he was not looking forward to this exercise on a regular basis. His feet were sore even though he had two pairs of socks on to fit the boots.

He slept like a log that night after the dinner that was too large. His mates were all hungry and enjoying his leftovers. The pudding was stewed apple which he shared with his new friends; he did not like the look of the custard and was not too keen on the apple. The tea was too strong it nearly curdled the milk, at least there was plenty of sugar.

The next day after marching for about one hour they were sent to the firing range. Charley had never handled a rifle before and he was given this large Enfield 303. Luckily they were firing from the prone position so he did not have to take the full weight. They were shown how to fire and reload and warned they had live ammunition. They all loaded while the sergeant watched. A couple had problems but when every gun was loaded they were told to take the prone position. Again, a couple of soldiers had to be told about the prone position. The rest of the group jumped straight down but Charley stood looking at the target. He visualized it as a diamond with a flaw in the middle; he had to hit the flaw.

His first shot hit the target but to the left hand side. He now carefully adjusted the rifle and his second shot was a bull's eye. He then took his time and the next four shots hit the bull or very close to it. He was the last to shoot and his mates were standing around clapping. The sergeant was shaking his head and telling the men to be quiet.

"Are you sure you have never fired a rifle before?"

"No sarge, I see the bull's eye as a diamond and have to hit the flaw in the middle. This rifle is a bit heavy but lying down takes most of the weight."

The sergeant did not understand the first remark but told Charley to report to him first thing in the morning when he would square it with the drill sergeant. That was great news for Charley.

He was now the most popular private in the barracks, they still enjoyed sharing his dinner but his shooting had them spellbound. His mates asked him what he meant about the diamond. He explained all he knew about gemstones and then he was bombarded with personal jewellery. Everyone wanted to know about their rings and necklaces. One man had a ring of eighteen carat gold and Charley advised him to keep it for special occasions as it could easily get scratched or distorted. He had the whole troop in the palm of his hand along with their jewellery. Most of it had cheap stones but a couple of the rings had good stones and he advised the owners to take care of their possessions.

The next day he reported to the firing range. The sergeant told him to try from the kneeling position. After the first shot he was hitting the bull every time. Then the sergeant told him to try from the standing position. Although he was hitting the target the rifle was too heavy.

"Sir, I am a slow shooter and the longer I hold the rifle the more I tremble; maybe you have a lighter rifle."

"Yes, I understand. Try this 202, it is much lighter. We have it available but we do not often use it. Actually we have many different model rifles but if you are posted abroad they may not have as many."

No matter what position he was in, Charley was hitting the bull regularly.

"Here, now try this FAL rifle. It is made in Belgium but I think it is the best available. Use it for single shot only."

He was shown how to load the rifle and how to shoot single shot. Charley liked the feel of this gun and after a couple of shots he was hitting the target regularly no matter what position he was using. This gun felt comfortable in his small hands.

"Sarge, I like the feel of this gun. Can I take it home?"

"You certainly cannot, you cheeky bugger."

They were all smiles when an officer approached. They both stood to attention and saluted. The officer had been watching unseen by Charley and the sergeant: he told them to fall out.

"Young man, I think you might be one of the better shots in the army and if we were at war you would be a sniper. Well done, private. Please carry on."

Charley thought about that compliment and realised in a war he would be shooting at people not targets. That gave him a weird feeling. The sergeant was allowing him target practice every day and that became a minor relief from marching. He tried all sorts of guns including some ancient ones but his favourite was the FAL rifle.

They completed their training and all were fair shots. After a couple of months word came that his cohort was heading to Cyprus. All his mates were very excited. Cyprus is where Charley met Trevor, his soon to be good friend and leader. The troop had to get a map from the library to locate Cyprus. Then someone suggested it could be hot in their new camp. Everyone was in a good mood; they did not realize that exertion in a hot humid climate could be energy draining. They were all dreaming of sand, sea and sunshine and looking forward to leaving cold Aldershot. Charley's gunnery sergeant was also jealous as he had no chance of leaving Aldershot. Charley asked him whether there was a war in Cyprus; he had visions of being a sniper and having to kill people. The sergeant told him there was a bit of civilian unrest and he would probably not have to shoot at anyone. It was on Charley's record that he be issued with a 202 or a FAL rifle. On leaving the camp he thanked the sergeant for making his time at Aldershot a pleasant one. The sergeant thanked him for displaying the best shooting he had seen from a recruit.

The train journey to Portsmouth was full of merriment. They were all excited about going to sea; many of them had never seen the sea. No one had been on a large ship and the sight of the ships in the harbour had then all reciting the phrase, *I came to the sea to see the sea and now I can see the sea*. They lined up at the station and were taken to the dock by lorry.

They embarked on a troop ship with two other groups and quickly mingled with the other soldiers. It appeared that the other two groups were going to Aden and again no one had any idea of the location of Aden. Their quarters were fairly spacious being meant for more soldiers. Each man had two kits, Arthur had made Charley his second kit and it fitted better than the first. They had also found smaller boots. Arthur was glad to leave Aldershot as he thought he would be held back to modify uniforms. Charley now felt comfortable in his new uniform and he, too was glad to leave cold Aldershot.

On the first morning on board ship they lined up for parade and it was blowing a gale. Several men dropped out of line to be sick, with the instruction not to vomit against the wind. Of course it had to happen to one fellow and the troop had to suppress their laughter. The wind was cold and they had to stay on deck to exercise. Charley got a cushy job helping Arthur adjust some uniforms. He was happy to cut cloth rather than do push-ups on the deck.

As they approached Gibraltar the wind dropped and the weather became warmer. The whole troop was now enjoying the exercise on the deck. Charley wanted the uniform adjustment to come to an end. Arthur was thinking that he could put tailoring in a force eight gale in his work record. Everyone was eating a full meal and Charley's leftovers were in demand. Charley was praising the cooks so he was getting bigger portions and that made him very popular.

As they approached Cyprus they were wishing their newfound friends goodbye as they were going to be on the sea a few more days. They were going through the Suez Canal and although they wanted to leave the ship some of Charley's troop was envious at not seeing one of the wonders of the world (at least that was what they were told). The troop had expected to dock in the port but the ship anchored off the coast and they took a tender directly to their barracks. Most of the troop were uncomfortable with the tender being tossed by the sea but it was only a short journey. Getting off the tender they had a sight of their new barracks. This was a fantastic barracks; one side was a beach that excited the troop. They were taken to a hut and introduced to Lance Corporal Trevor who was going to bunk with them and explain the situation. The huts were fitted with fans and had their own shower room. One bloke thought it was like a good hotel by the seaside.

"Sit on your bunks and please listen."
Charley was surprised Trevor said please.

"We are here to keep two potentially warring factions apart. The Greek Cypriots want to unite with Greece and the Turkish Cypriots see that as killing their rights. We are in the middle and are trying to keep the two factions apart. So far there has been no real violence in our area but there is potential for these demonstrations to get violent. You will be given a baton and shield and man either side of a barrier. The baton is to be swung to keep the protesters at bay, preferably not hitting anyone. These protesters are middle aged and old although there are a few young activists. Their average height is about the same as Charley's so unless there is real problem I hope you won't hit anyone. You will not be armed but the officers will have pistols. Do you have any questions?"

"How can we tell who is Greek or who is Turkish?"

"The officer will identify the flags they are waving and if he gets it wrong I'll tell you."

The troop liked his sense of humour.

"Tomorrow you will have the day off to acclimatize; sometimes I think the army is almost human. Beware of the sun, I am sure you will all go to the beach and most of you will get sunburnt. Heat stroke can be considered a self-inflicted wound so do not get a black mark on your record. Now all get a good night's sleep."

"What about food?"

"Oh yes, I forgot, I hope they have some left in the canteen. I assume you will eat everything available."

"We are not fussy as long as it is good grub and plenty of it," said one of the soldiers.

The next day after inspection then breakfast they were all rushing to the beach under the watchful eye of Trevor. He was smiling to himself; they were just like little kids rushing to the sea. Most were wearing the shorts issued to them in Aldershot but some were swimming in their underpants. Trevor was sitting in the shade and it was not long before Charley appeared putting on his shirt.

"That sun is bloody hot and anyway I can't swim. When my friends went to the baths they would not take me as they might lose me and I would surely drown. I like the water here but I think a large wave will wash me away."

Trevor had a good laugh at that remark.

"Would you like to go to the firing range? I have seen your record and would like to see for myself. There is a lifeguard and I hope no one drowns while we are away."

"Yes, please, that is the place I feel at home. I'd never fired a rifle before Aldershot but now I love the feel of one in my hands. I think my record will be good as the sergeant liked me."

They walked to the rifle range where Charley was introduced to the sergeant in charge. Trevor told him that Charley was a good shot and he wanted to check out his ability.

The sergeant looked at Charley and asked what gun he would like. He looked at Charley and commented that at his height Charley should not be in the army but he was here.

"If I am in the lying down position I will use a 303 probably the best for accuracy. In other positions I would use a 202 or the FAL."

"Sounds like you are not a novice. Here is a 303 let's see what you can do."

The next six bullets hit the bull's eye and then with the FAL there was the same result.

The sergeant raised his eyebrows and said, "I have not seen anyone do that on this range before. Can you do that tomorrow?"

"I think I can, sarge."

Trevor and Charley thanked the sergeant and walked back to the beach. Some of the troop now had their shirts on and were sitting in the shade.

"I now know you can shoot and I want you to have a special duty tomorrow. We will be going to a road that connects two villages, one Greek one Turkish. These are farming villages and we are there to keep the villagers apart. So far these demonstrations have been peaceful but in the cities there has been violence. You will be on top of a lorry at the end of our barricade. A spotter with binoculars will be with you. There will be a similar pair of men at the other end of the line. You will be facing the Greeks and if you see anyone with a gun you are allowed to disable him or her." Charley said, "You mean I can shoot at a woman; I am not sure whether I can. Surely no woman will carry a gun."

"Look, any woman with a gun can probably use it and possibly use it better than her male compatriots. She will be shooting at your mates who are only armed with batons and shields. I am afraid an armed civilian of either sex has to be your target."

"Okay, Trevor I just pray I do not have to shoot anyone. I will try not to kill anyone either male or female."

"One other thing it can get pretty hot on top of the lorry so drink plenty of water. We are lucky most of the demonstrators here are old, but farmers always have guns. If you have to shoot, hit the lower abdomen or the shoulder, an injured assailant will be useful for information."

Trevor gathered the men and told them that after lunch they would have some practice using their batons and shields. There were a lot of red faces and bodies and the food consumption was lower than normal. Charley smiled when his leftovers were refused. The troop soon found that wielding their batons for about half an hour was exhausting in the heat.

"Hey, this is hard work. I was sweating before I started and now it's dripping from my nose," said one of the soldiers.

Trevor replied that they should not put much effort into swinging the baton unless things got ugly. The swinging batons were designed to keep the villagers back from the barrier.

The next day the troop went to the barricade to relieve the night patrol. There were lots of sore bodies but no one wanted to be relieved through sickness. Trevor smiled as he lined up a group of red faced men either side of the barricade. He showed Charley which way to point his gun and told him the metal parts would get very hot in the sun. Charley was helped climb on top of the lorry. After a couple of hours the men were getting restless and Trevor was allowing them to take shade occasionally. Charley and his mate had no shade but plenty of water.

After a couple of hours they heard shouting and as though the two groups were synchronized, they appeared at the same time. Trevor told his men that demonstrations were planned after breakfast and they all ate breakfast at the same time. The groups approached the soldiers but stopped well clear of the swinging batons. They were waving flags and shouting slogans (and probably insults) at each other. Charley could see that many of the men had walking sticks but he could not spot a gun. His mate with the binoculars was unhappy no one was armed but Charley was relieved. After about half an hour the demonstrators seemed to drift away. Charley could see no young people and particularly no young girls. At lunch time the squad was relieved by another squad and they were all happy to stop swinging their batons. Later in the day they went back to the barricade but everything was quiet.

Charley said to Trevor, "As I lay there with a loaded gun I started to think of my mother and grandparents, I was scared stiff I might have to fire. I looked at both sides and they were all old."

"Yes, if we were not there they might beat each other to death with walking sticks."

Charley laughed but realised he would be doing the same tomorrow. This went on for several weeks and although there was violence elsewhere these farmers just wanted to shout and wave flags. The demonstrations died down and Trevor received word that his squad was leaving Cyprus. They were going to Aden by plane.

After dinner Trevor had the squad line up in the billet and he carried out his inspection. This was unusual and the squad sensed there was something about to happen. Trevor ordered them to pick up their rifles and make sure they were unloaded. He then went around and inspected each rifle and took particular attention to Charley's FAL. Although the squad was silent there was an air of anticipation. Trevor then told them to fall out as he had something to tell them. They were all ears, the anticipation was killing them.

"Tomorrow we will be flying to Aden on a RAF transport plane. You will have your rifles and ammunition but the rifles will be unloaded as we do not want anyone making a hole in the plane by accident."

"Where is Aden?"

"Let me finish. Aden is at the southern end of the Red Sea and to get there we would normally go through the Suez Canal, I have a map you can look at in a minute. We have had an easy time here in Cyprus as I can see by your suntans but I am told Aden is more violent. Our job will be to keep protestors from doing damage to installations: I have no idea what installations."

Charley piped up, "I have never flown and I am scared of flying, I am already starting to sweat."

"The army does not understand the term scared. I have never flown and I think every member of this squad has not flown. I am apprehensive but I have faith in the RAF."

"What is apprehensive?"

"It's a sort of feeling in the stomach because it is unknown, I am not worried but a little uneasy. I have to obey orders so I can forget my feelings. You all have to forget your fears. The RAF are not going to let us down. They are all well trained and I don't think our opponents in Aden have fighter planes."

There was silence before everyone gathered around the map, they all agreed no one had flown before. Trevor was looking at them. A few were suntanned and Charley had tanned well. Others were as white as when they arrived. They were a happy bunch and many liked that Trevor talked to them in a simple way. Trevor was hoping the RAF would give them a smooth flight.

"I don't like heights," said Charley.

Trevor said, "I don't think you will have a window seat and I have been told there will be no windows. It will be like sitting in a bus with the windows blacked out. Have a good night's sleep, you will see another country tomorrow. Let's hope our job is as cushy as this one."

The next morning the squad lined up and was transported to the airfield. Trevor sensed their anxiety. No one said a word but Trevor was thinking how he could break the tension. To break the mood Trevor said that Charley had a good tan and some of the others had no tan at all. He told them that it might be hereditary and Charley probably had Mediterranean blood. That stirred them up but then they were ordered to board the plane. They filed into the back of the plane and took their seats. They were then ordered to fasten their harness and one of the crew showed them how. While they were taxiing down the runway Charley asked about Mediterranean blood. This was the distraction Trevor wanted.

"I know you are all from England but do you know where your great grand parents came from? How far can you trace your family back?"

This started everyone talking and they forgot about take-off and landing. Trevor was engaged in talking with Charley. They both had little knowledge of their lineage before their grand-parents. In fact only one soldier knew his great grand-parents. The landing was smooth and no one really noticed as they could see nothing and they were all involved in conversation. As the rear door opened they could all feel the heat and humidity. They were in full uniform with long trousers.

As they lined up on the tarmac an officer approached and said there had been a change in plan and they would be going to Kenya on a transport ship. They would stay overnight in the barracks and would board the ship the next day. The barracks was cool and they had time to study maps that Trevor had found in the library.

Charley again was the one to ask questions.

"Kenya is in Africa. Will we see lions and tigers?"

"You may see lions but there are no tigers in Africa."

This had the squad roaring with laughter. Trevor left them to talk to one of the officers. It seemed that Trevor's squad was being used as a relief troop and the officer thought they would be back in Aden later in the year. The officer told Trevor about the Mau Mau but he thought that the problem had died down and probably the troops they were relieving would come to Aden. They would go to Mombasa and then they could go anywhere in Kenya

The next day the squad was taken to the port and embarked on their transport ship. It seemed to be cooler and their cabins looked better than any barracks they had occupied. While they settled in Trevor spoke to a naval officer who could give him information on their upcoming voyage. He wanted to tell his soldiers what they could expect. He accosted a junior officer and before he knew it he was facing the captain on the bridge. This was an impressive room and Trevor was looking all around. There seemed to be dials everywhere and he could not see a steering wheel. He saluted as the captain approached.

"Well, soldier, I understand from your accent you are from Birmingham, meet a fellow Brummie, me. I am told you want to know where we are going. Do you read maps?"

"Yes, sir, but the maps I normally read are land maps but I will try my best to read yours."

Trevor could not believe what was happening. The captain sat with him explaining their journey to Mombasa. They would not stop at any other port. He ordered tea and they sat discussing Birmingham. The captain explained that there seemed too few Brummies in the navy. Most of his men were from areas along the coast but there were a few from inland areas. Trevor asked why he was brought straight to the captain.

"I always watch soldiers coming on to my ship. You lined them up and said something. They all started smiling and that continued as they boarded. I don't know what you said and I would like to know. A happy ship is an easy ship."

"Well, we arrived in Aden by plane. None of my men had ever flown, including me, and they were apprehensive. There were no windows so they could not see take-off or landing. I told them this time they would see everything and to enjoy the experience. I also told them praying was not necessary; that was what made them smile."

"I like that you put them at ease, are you a regular?" asked the captain.

"Yes, sir, I joined up before conscription. Most of my squad are conscripts but I am sure some will sign on. I told them to join the army and see the world; that was why I joined."

"You do credit to the army."

"Thank you, sir, may I borrow a couple of maps as I always like to keep my squad informed? They are at least getting an education in geography. I am also trying to educate them in other subjects as well."

The captain motioned yes and shook his head as Trevor left the bridge. This man was a leader. Trevor went straight to the quarters and spread out the maps. Charley was first to ask, "how come the captain talks to you?"

"He is a Brummie so next question."

The whole troop was interested in the maps and amazed at the size of Africa when everything was explained in miles. Trevor explained they would go straight to Mombasa and would not stop at any other port. Their quarters were very comfortable, as the voyage was smooth and no one was sea sick. The squad had some exercise but most of the time they were gazing at the sea and were amazed at the fish life. Charley and Arthur spent most of their time in the sewing room and Arthur was instructing some sailors in tailoring. Trevor was very happy and had many conversations with the captain. He also had a few conversations with the army officers on board. They were flummoxed by Trevor's access to the captain and a little jealous. Trevor asked whether they might have a firing competition if the captain could select his best shot in his crew. They would have to set up a target at the stern and of course the rocking of the ship would make it a moving target. The captain was very interested and selected one of his officers. Of course Charley was selected with his trusty FAL.

There was great excitement in the ship and a target was constructed and mounted on the stern. The sailor said he would prefer to fire a 303 in the kneeling position. Charley said he would fire his FAL in the same position. The captain suggested that the first shot should not count so they could get adjusted to the motion of the ship. Charley thought that a good idea as his first shot was just outside the bull, his next six shots hit the bull and the sailor admitted defeat.

The captain came close to Trevor and quietly said, "Cunning bugger."

"It might be good for morale to have a shoot-off regularly as Charley is an exception," said Trevor.

The captain thought that a very good idea. He also wanted all his crew to learn to shoot. Trevor told him that was a good idea. Charley and Trevor were invited to the bridge and each given a glass of rum. Charley asked for water as he did not drink, which brought laughter from the sailors on the bridge. In the dormitory Charley was the toast of the town (cabin). All his mates crowded around slapping him on the back.

They disembarked at Mombasa and the whole troop saluted the captain. He smiled and wished them well. They were escorted to the train station and an awaiting train. They were in open lorries and on the way they saw many people, all black. At one stage they were in a traffic jam next to a market. There were plenty of stalls but traderswere sitting on the ground with their fruit and vegetables spread out before them. It was all very colourful and the squad were amazed at the sight. On the train they had two separate carriages to themselves. They were all glad when the train started moving as the heat and humidity was like Aden. Two soldiers in each carriage were ordered to load their rifles in case of trouble. Charley was an obvious choice and Trevor also had a loaded rifle. There was an officer with a loaded pistol. Trevor made sure every man could load his rifle quickly; he told them he did not know the situation but best to be prepared. Trevor had no idea of the current situation in Kenya and the officer was also ignorant of the current news. The big question was whether the Mau Mau were active along the railway line.

Trevor ordered that they could watch the scenery but no man was to put his head outside the window. They were all told to be seated and if there was trouble to duck under the tables.

"We don't want to give anyone target practice and if they have a shooter like Charley we could be handling a headless body."

There was nervous laughter around the squad in the first carriage and Trevor repeated his order to the second carriage.

Charley said, "Do you remember that train journey from Mombasa to Nairobi? It was magical. I had never seen ·so many animals. After that everything went downhill and Kenya was a disappointment. The only other good thing was the climate."

"Yes, I remember that journey; for once I had no idea of the situation. I was very apprehensive and I agree that train journey was the best. I would like to go back to Africa and let Li see some of those amazing sights. I gather Kenya is now a tourist place but I hope they have cleaned up some of those horrible sights we saw."

"Yes, I have talked about Africa to Nur but she tells me we have to go to England first. I just love the way our wives have hit it off. I think we married two smart ladies."

At Nairobi station they were met and escorted to their barracks. From the lorries they could see very few white people. Trevor and his escort officer were taken to the camp commander. He told them that the morning duty would be as guards for the internment camp and in the afternoon the squad would patrol the squatter camps. The commander described them as the worst slums he had ever seen. The white Kenyans and many of the local Kikuyus wanted them cleared but he did not have the manpower. Trevor thought of slums and that took him back to Birmingham. He was later to see these as shanty towns for the poor which were much worse than any Birmingham slums.

At the prison camps they patrolled the perimeter with loaded rifles. Charley hated this guard duty, he saw poorly clothed prisoners lining up for food. They looked beaten in spirit and most had their heads bowed. He could not tell whether they had been physically beaten but they were certainly beaten mentally. The morning duty was a piece of cake compared to the afternoon duty.

The squatter camps were the worst places he had ever seen and made Charley physically sick. He saw poor families with skinny children and everyone looked half starved. The stench and the sights turned his stomach. That started him thinking about the way other people lived. Cyprus had rich areas with grandiose villas and even the rural villages looked liveable but these places were indescribable. He could not understand why the authorities could not clear these camps. He was not privy to Trevor's information.

The tour in Kenya only lasted a couple of months and they were informed they were going back to Aden. Both Charley and Trevor were very relieved to get out of Nairobi. They had seen very little of the city. They had heard of the Norfolk hotel but could never get there; as ordinary soldiers they may not have been let in. It was barracks to prison camp, back to barracks then to the squatter camps followed by back to barracks. It seemed to Trevor and Charley that they were not allowed into the city. It was a miserable time for the whole squad and they were all happy to leave Kenya.

Again the RAF was going to transport them. Charley was disappointed as he would love to have gone on the train journey to Mombasa. The rest of the squad were also disappointed, they liked a leisurely cruise. Apparently the protests in Aden had intensified and reinforcements were required. The squad was resigned to flying not sailing. They were now looking forward to their flight although a bit apprehensive about Aden. The climate in Nairobi was very pleasant compared with their limited memories of Aden. Trevor gave them all the information he could get from the officers. He learned this was much more serious than Cyprus and some of the demonstrators were armed and grenades had been used. Charley realised that Trevor was very protective of this squad.

They landed in Aden and were taken to the barracks. There were a lot of people on the street but as they did not understand the language they could not judge whether the shouts were hostile. Much of the city looked poor, they were in covered lorries but they could see through the back as they drove along. At the barracks Trevor had to talk to the commander. Trevor returned from a briefing with the news that they were to protect the Post Office. The squad would be behind a barricade. They would have shields and batons and their rifles would be stacked behind the second row of men, this row would have their rifles at the ready. Trevor hoped that would be a quiet place like they had in Cyprus, but little did he know that the Post Office was a big symbol of the occupation. This was not going to be a cushy job.

Trevor called Charley and a man called Terry to have a chat. They were going to be snipers on the balconies of the Post Office. They would each have a spotter and they had instructions to shoot to kill if they saw anyone throw a grenade. The squad would be behind the barrier with shields but any rock throwers were fair game. Trevor advised they move around on the balconies just in case the protesters had a sniper. An officer would also be on each balcony surveying what was happening. The Post Office was quite a substantial building and Charley thought that any other time he would have liked a tour of the building.

The next morning the squad relieved the night watch. They lined up in two groups and waited for the demonstrators. Charley picked his balcony and fixed his firing positions. Arthur was the spotter and he found two chairs. Nothing happened for a while and the officer said it would all start after breakfast. So far that sounded similar to Cyprus but they were to find these demonstrations to be more intense.

Sure enough a crowd gathered at about eight a.m. There was some shouting but little movement. Then a group with a banner arrived and the crowd moved closer to the barrier. Charley and Arthur were watching and Arthur was looking for any armed men. The front of the crowd stopped about ten feet in front of the barrier and some men came forward to throw stones.

The officer said, "Those men will come forward and retreat after throwing their stones. Do you think you could fire at about the area where their front feet land?"

Charley fired and hit the ground in front of the protesters. Suddenly it went quiet for a while and then the rock throwers came back.

"Do you think you could shoot one of the throwers in the leg?"

"Yes, sir, I will shoot one in the foot."

He did so and the downed man was pulled back into the mob which was retreating. Charley moved firing position and asked the officer if he could shoot at the banner.

"Certainly I think today's demonstration may be fizzling out."

Charley shot a hole in the flag and then shot one of the holding posts which collapsed. The crowd quickly dispersed. The officer was pleased and said he would recommend Charley get a medal.

The next few weeks were less intense than the first morning. Charley told the officer that there seemed to be a group who wanted to incite the mob and without them the protests were mainly peaceful. Trevor had also reported that observation. There was more trouble in other parts of Aden and Charley was hoping that he would not have to shoot anyone again. Of course this lull was about to change. Information was that a group would attack the Post Office and Trevor's squad should be ready.

Charley was introduced to a new officer who told them he had no qualms about killing demonstrators. Again some stone throwers came forward and Charley put a couple of shots in front of the mob. The officer frowned but the stone throwing stopped. Then Arthur spotted someone light a Molotov cocktail but before Charley could shoot the cocktail was on its way. Charley then shot the man in the shoulder and saw another man lighting a cocktail. He shot the bottle and flaming petrol went everywhere catching several bystanders. The officer was jumping for joy and that section of the crowd quickly dispersed. The officer noted it in his report.

Weeks and months went by and the squad was getting fed up of Aden. Charley had injured a few protesters but never had to kill anyone. He was happy that all the protesters were men; he did not have to shoot at a woman. The interesting thing was that the Molotov cocktail incident had never been reported to Trevor and Charley had never told him the story. The incident occurred at about the time when the far end of the barricade had been attacked and Trevor was busy marshalling his squad.

Trevor was able to get into the ear of one of the commanders telling him his troop was exhausted. Charley was over the moon when he was informed they were to be relieved and sent to Singapore. He went to the library and showed the troop its location. Trevor was surprised when they all seemed to know about Singapore until Charley showed him the map. Trevor congratulated Charley for having initiative. Trevor warned that the climate might be similar to Aden but maybe not as hot.

Leaving Aden was a great pleasure for Charley; he even re-enlisted as did many of the squad. Although the weather was rough Charley was a good sailor but no one wanted to share his excess food. They had good conditions on the ship but they still had to march and do exercises. Trevor told them he was not sure what to expect but they had to keep fit. He had heard of the Malay incursion but knew few details.

"When you told me in Cyprus I might have to shoot a woman I was petrified. That first day I lay on the lorry I could think of nothing else. In Kenya I was praying that none of the prisoners tried to escape as I might have to shoot them. The prisoners looked so miserable and cowed I might have missed on purpose. Aden was different as the officer ordered me to shoot a stone thrower's leg and I did not think. Then when I shot the Molotov cocktail thrower it came without thought."

"When was that?"

"Arthur identified a man throwing a Molotov cocktail and I shot him in the shoulder, he would never throw again. Then I shot the bottle of a second thrower and it showered the bystanders with burning petrol. You should have seen them scatter. That killed the demonstration."

"I never knew, there was no report of that action. There should have been a record and it should have been in your record."

"The officer noted it and I assumed you would see the report."

"You should have received a medal and I wonder if the officer claimed it was all his doing."

"No good looking back, we are now both in civvies and good riddance to the army."

Charley was aware of Trevor's problem with the army.

Arriving in Singapore the band was playing on the dock, Charley noted that many of the bagpipe players were too dark to be Scottish. It was something to be welcomed and it stuck in Charley's memory. They filed off onto the dock and Charley thought it was hot but not as hot as Aden. The street scene was different but looked cleaner. Their barracks were clean and although the temperature and humidity were similar to Aden the fans seemed to work better. Charley slept like a log and had to be woken for inspection the next day. Suddenly everything was so relaxed and all Charley could do was smile. He still had images of Nairobi and they would not go away for a long time.

After a bit of marching Sergeant Trevor took him to the firing range. This was a relief for Charley, he could not think of a better spot. The sergeant in charge of the firing range asked, "Aren't you too small for the army?"

"Yes, sir, but they would not give me time off to grow."

"Your sergeant tells me you are a pretty good shot so we shall see. What gun would you like to use?"

"If I am lying down then a 303, any other position I will take either a 202 or FAL."

"May I chose any model?"

"Yes."

"Then give me what you have."

"Let's try this old 303. I don't think it has been used for a while.

It used to be standard issue and one I used regularly."

"Do you mind if I take a trial shot."

"No son, have a go."

Charley hit the bull first shot and said, "This is a good old beauty."

Charley then hit the bull with the next five shots. The sergeant's eyes lit up.

"I would have to search out a 202 but here is a FAL."

Charley's next shots hit the bull.

"No one has ever shot like that on this range. You are welcome back any day and I will arrange an audience."

During the next few weeks Charley gave an exhibition and his squad was very happy. They enjoyed a bit of free time watching Charley shoot. Of course they were still sharing his leftovers. Then one day an order came from on high that there were to be no more demonstrations. Trevor talked to an officer who said that one of the senior brass did not like an ordinary soldier showing his expertise. Trevor told Charley what he had heard and Charley's response had Trevor laughing.

"The army is full of absurdities and most come from the officers."

"Where did you get absurdities from?"

"I bought a dictionary and wanted to use a new word, so you can see I have not got very far."

Charley was enjoying Singapore but he knew it could not last. The troop was told that they were going into Malay to protect the rubber plantations. None of them had any idea about rubber plantations but they were going to enjoy a train ride. Trevor was in charge of loading them on to the first two carriages. They had unloaded rifles until the officer disappeared to his better carriage, then Trevor told them to reload their rifles. Charley asked Trevor why they should be armed. Trevor said he had a bad feeling about this trip.

Everything was going smoothly until the train hit the brakes. Trevor ordered them to take cover. Charley had no problem getting under the table in front of him. Suddenly there was rapid fire that smashed all the windows. This was the first time anyone had shot at Charley, actually the fire was indiscriminate but Charley thought it was meant for him. He wanted to take aim at who was firing but Trevor told him to keep his head down.

Trevor told them to fire their rifles through the broken windows but not to show themselves. Charley was by a window divide and could see the bush. He fired several shots and thought he hit someone. Trevor ordered the firing to stop and the second fireman came in to report that the driver and the senior fireman had been killed. The fireman had hidden in the coal. Now Trevor wanted someone to go on top of the carriage to see if there were any terrorists still active. Finally, Charley volunteered as he did not want his sergeant to go. Charley thought as the smallest he would make the most difficult target. As he was scaling the ladder to get on the carriage roof he was praying there was not a good shot out there. Once on the roof he flattened and surveyed the bush on the left hand side. He could see no movement but there was a body on the edge of the bush. About ten feet past the bush edge was a line of trees but he could see no movement there. He could see no movement anywhere else so he switched his gaze to the right hand side. There appeared to be no cover near the train and he could see no movement. After reporting to Trevor he was ordered to come down from the roof.

Trevor was afraid the engine might build up too much pressure so he sent a couple of soldiers with the fireman along the right side to check the engine. He then asked Charley to cover him as he went to take a look at the body. About halfway to the body Trevor flattened and stopped. Charley crawled up close to Trevor to take a better look. Trevor pointed to a second body; Charley confirmed he could not see any movement. They crawled slowly towards the body. The first dead man was shot in the neck and the second man had been shot twice. Charley looked at these poorly clothed peasants and felt sorry for them. His thoughts went back to the prison camp in Kenya and poorly clothed prisoners.

Many people from the other parts of the train descended on the scene. Trevor was angry and ordered his troop back into their carriages. He called them sightseers and Charley agreed. Luckily there was an army doctor who examined the bodies. It looked like Charley had shot the second man in the chest, evidenced by the types of bullet. This was the man who had been put out of his misery by his friends. Trevor kept his men inside the train until an officer ordered them to clear the lines. Charley stood on the front of the engine while his troop cleared the tracks and then off they continued to their destination.

They shared a barracks with Malay troops many of whom spoke English. None of Trevor's troop spoke anything but English. They went out on patrol together to visit the rubber plantations. Some of the managers were British and could give information about terrorists in the area. The insurgency had gone quiet and the workers were happy to see the terrorists leave. As one worker put it, "They came from the north and were armed and we could not stop them. We are glad they left but if you find any shoot them."

The rubber plantations were so orderly and Charley was seeing trees all in one line. He was not used to this. There were not too many trees in Birmingham or any of the other places he had visited. There were two clubs in the area with European and Malay members and Trevor and Charley loved visiting both. One had a football field and the troop loved to have a kick around. The other was preparing a cricket pitch as one of the local Sultans loved cricket. Both clubs loved having the soldiers as the bar takings were very healthy. Trevor and Charley liked the one with the cricket pitch as it was quieter and looked on to one of the plantations. A cold beer late in the afternoon on the verandah was a very pleasant experience. There was an abundance of birds and plenty smiling and waving Malays walking by to keep their attention.

After a couple of months with little activity the troop was ordered back to Singapore. All the squad had enjoyed lots of recreation and peace. They were loath to return to the city although most were city boys.

Back in Singapore they had free time and Trevor visited a café to chat with university students. Charley went along and loved to look at the female students. He was intimidated as their English was better than his. Suddenly Trevor was transferred to Hong Kong and Charley was promoted to corporal. He thought he must be the smallest corporal in the army but he never had trouble with his troop. Some officers had been watching him and although he was small he seemed to have the respect of the privates and so they recommended his promotion.

Trevor had been gone about a month and one afternoon Charley decided to visit the coffee shop. He told the students he could not discuss politics and they asked him to tell them about England. His knowledge of England was limited to Birmingham but the students loved his stories. He told them about having a bath in the living room in front of a coal fire. He described a large tin bath and they were all laughing. There was laughter when he told them about outside toilets in the winter; they all agreed that no one had ever told them about slums. Charley had not seen there was a female student in the audience and when he noticed her he was embarrassed. He told them about working for a jeweller and how they had taught him about gold and precious stones. Some of the male students said they had a party to attend and wished him well. Suddenly he was left with the female student and she was so good looking he had to try his best not to stare. She said she was interested in what he had said about precious stones; her father traded in lots of things including precious stones. Her name was Nur and she was Malay. Her spoken English was almost perfect and she said she liked Charley's accent. Charley apologized for his Brummie accent, she said she loved it but was confused with a few words and phrases.

"What is a two up two down house? What is a coal house and what is a cut? I also noticed some words I think ended in a 'g' but you say the words without a 'g' I hope you are not offended by this observation."

Charley could never be offended by any observation Nur had. Now he relaxed, he could answer those questions easily. He also explained Brummagem and the Black Country. Many words were spoken differently to the way they were spelt and dropping the 'g' was common. They chatted for a while and before she left Nur asked if it was all right if she asked her father whether he would like to talk to Charley about precious stones. She asked if they could meet in a couple of days at the café. Charley's head was spinning; the most beautiful girl was making a date. Of course he replied in the affirmative. That night he could hardly sleep thinking of Nur. He had only really seen her face but if the rest was as beautiful he was lucky to know her.

Charley was at the café early and on his second coffee before Nur arrived. She told him her dad would like to talk about precious stones but he was busy at present. Charley could not care less, he was sitting with an angel. They chatted about his impression of Singapore. Charley was diplomatic but admitted he liked up-country Malaya better. She was intrigued as she had never been out of Singapore. Charley remembered that before Antwerp he had never been outside Birmingham. Nur said she had many relatives in Malaya and now she wanted to go north. Charley told her about the rubber plantations and how he loved the peace and quiet except of course for the bird songs. Nur was really enjoying the conversation and hoped they could meet the next day. Charley could not believe his luck he had another date. This was something new to him and he loved every minute.

Finally after a few more dates Nur told him her father had free time and Charley should come to tea. He had almost forgotten about meeting her father. Nur escorted him to her home which was a large house for Singapore. He was introduced to Nur's father and mother and shook their hands; he was unsure what to say. They sat and had tea and a cake then it was down to business. They were ushered into the father's study with the largest desk Charley had ever seen. A purple pouch and an open box were produced and the father poured out twenty-five diamonds into the box. Now Charley could relax. He had only uttered about four words but now he could look at diamonds. There was silence as he sorted the diamonds into three groups; he rather enjoyed the silence. When he had finished, he pointed to the first pile and said, "Good quality stones, well cut, but a little small. The second pile has good stones but, in my opinion, not well cut. The third pile has interesting stones in that they have flaws and one has an inclusion. These could be as valuable as the well-cut stones, I think there is a market for these stones but I am not an expert on the market."

Charley then told them about the growth of diamonds and how bits of rock could get trapped. He also told Nur's father that these ill-formed diamonds needed more examination by specialists. Nur's father made no comment but produced two more pouches and put each pile into a separate pouch. Nur was smiling but Charley was expecting some kind of response. Finally the father thanked Charley and wished him good evening.

Nur escorted Charley back to the barracks and said he had made a good impression. Charley was thinking the opposite but he had enjoyed the evening and hoped it would not be the last.

"My father rarely sits still and says nothing. If he had disagreed with you, he would have said something or have snorted. I saw the way he looked at you and the diamond piles and he liked what he saw. Now are you free for coffee tomorrow?"

This was unbelievable, he had another date. Charley knew he was going back into Malaya. He told Nur if he was not at the café at the normal time he would be travelling. She understood and said they should meet every afternoon that week. Charley was speechless, he had a date every day. On the Friday afternoon Charley was on a train travelling north. His troop had unloaded guns but he quietly told a few of the better shots to load their rifles. The train passed the station where they stopped last time; so they were going north. The train started to slow and Charley was on alert. He motioned to the troop to keep low just in case. As they were stopping an officer came through the carriage door to say there was a change in plan. They were going back to the garrison where they had previously stayed. Charley breathed a sigh of relief; he was expecting lots of bullets coming his way.

They were taken by lorries back to the barracks where they were welcomed by the new commandant. They had obviously made a good impression the last time they were there. Charley could never get over the beautiful English the Malay officers spoke. It was now back to patrolling the rubber plantations and meeting friends they had made before. Late one afternoon Charley was sitting with Arthur on the club verandah having a cold beer. Charley wished Nur was with him but Arthur was good company. Arthur had signed up with Charley as he wanted to assess whether he could set up a tailoring business in Singapore. He had come to the conclusion that the Indian tailors could undercut him so he was going to leave the army and go back to south London. Charley was wondering what he could do when his time came to leave the army. He had taken an auditing course and had a certificate. He was currently taking a part-time course in British and Singaporean taxation law. This was a difficult course but he enjoyed learning in his spare time; it also spared him some less desirable duties. The army was keen on the soldiers taking education courses and several of the officers were giving some lectures in local colleges. Many of his fellow students were advisers to Government MPs, a fact he only learned when they had a get together. Charley was a natural at making friends and that proved to be useful in the future.

Arriving back in Singapore he was delighted to find Nur at the café, he was wondering whether he would have to go to her house to meet her. She explained that secrets were hard to keep in Singapore and a trainload of troops returning from Malaya could never be kept secret. Again Charley enthused about Malaya and the beautiful countryside. Nur talked a little about her university course in Economics and then learned that Charley was taking a course in taxation law. She was very impressed and mentioned it to her father and he was very interested.

One afternoon Nur excused herself for leaving early as she had to meet a suitor who had been arranged by her parents. Charley said nothing but became very depressed; he had never had the courage to tell her he loved her. That night he had a fitful sleep. He could only see Nur walking away from him. The next day he went to the café half expecting not to see her. She showed up all smiles and Charley expected the worst.

"That last suitor was probably the worst. He wanted a kitchen wife and when I started to talk about women's positions in the world he was lost. He had no idea about foreign policy and knew almost nothing about local politics; even my mother could see he was entirely unsuitable. She is starting to say I am getting too old and should marry soon. The only man I want to marry is you. Would you marry me?"

Charley almost fell off his chair and Nur followed it up with a long kiss on the lips. All he could say was "Yes, please."

He then came to his senses and asked about her parents.

"I will deal with them and it could take a little time."

The café owner, a little Chinese man gave Charley the thumbs-up. Charley had no idea what he should do next but Nur took the initiative.

"I need to tell you about my family and I need to know a little about yours. I think you know I have two elder brothers, one is a manager for a French company and the younger one manages one of dad's shops. Before I met you I would have said my father's shop but I like dad. I am the youngest and my father, sorry dad, has always granted any wish I ask. You might think I am spoilt and like to get my own way but my eldest brother has taught me to have patience. My mother is more 'old school' and I have to outsmart her. I am the first in my family to go to University and my dad is proud of me and understands I will not be a traditional daughter. Many of our family live in Malaya and they are probably conservative and would not understand a daughter like me. I don't think my mother understands that yet; now how about you?"

Charley said, "I think I have told you I was basically brought up by my grandparents. I left school at fifteen. I went to work for a jeweller who was a great boss. He allowed me an afternoon off to do a course at a local college. This course was good but I learned more from the jewellers as they worked. I also did a couple of night courses. After I had been to Belgium to see a diamond workshop I had an interest in maps. Especially on a cold winter's morning or evening I would dream of living somewhere warm and exotic.

"My grandmother treated me more like a son. My grandfather treated me like a son and taught me many things including games which we played often. My mother came to live with them after my father left. He was a gambler and got into a lot of debt. I hate gambling and have never done it, my mother was deserted and I often hoped she would find a nice man. My father got lost and we have not seen him since, I think he might have a price on his head."

"How does a man get lost?"

"Well, he could have gone to another part of England and changed his name. We came from Manchester but I think the bookies would have found him there. Possibly he went to Scotland but that was probably too close. He could have gone to the continent but I don't think he spoke any other languages. America or Canada would seem the obvious places to get lost but if he continued his gambling he could be dead. He might even have gone to Australia. I think that would be far enough away. My father's sister lives in Manchester and I like her. I know very little about my extended family both on my mother's side and my dad's side."

"Do you think of him?"

"Yes, but I think of my mother and my grandparents more. I think I judged my father a long time ago and my opinion has not changed. I am not sure what I would say if I met him but it would not be nice. He destroyed my mother's life and that is unforgivable."

"I have a large family on both my dad's and mom's side. Many live in Malay but there are several families in Singapore. One of my cousins is a gambler and to me it is a disease and as such I can't make moral judgments."

Charley had new thoughts about his father but inside he was still angry, he still thought that gambling was something that could be given up. Leaving his mother who might have been harmed because of his gambling debts was unforgivable.

"I was conscripted into the army and ended up here, warm and exotic. One thing the army has done for me is to allow me to become more educated. I take courses at college that I could never take in England, I don't have the entry qualifications. I am sorry that story is a bit disjointed but I can answer any questions you have."

Nur said, "I will digest what you have told me and I am sure I will have questions in the future; I love the way you tell a story."

One day Nur asked Charley whether he knew about other precious stones as her dad had bought some new gems. She was not sure what stones he had but he would like Charley to look at them. Charley thought another visit to Nur's home was a good thing.

"One of the jewellers specialized in non-diamond precious stones and he showed me some good stones, but I am not an expert. I can tell badly cut stones and ones with flaws but I am not so good on colour. With some stones the colour is very important in setting the price."

"Would you come to tea and view some stones? I need you to impress my mother."

"How do I impress your mother?"

"My mother is a traditionalist and loves the royal family. She likes castles and large mansions."

"I am a Republican but I could talk about a bit of history I remember from school. I will have to do a bit of reading in the library."

"I am also a Republican but do your best."

Now Charley was on the spot; the only castle he had visited was at Dudley Zoo and he knew a little bit about how the royal family behaved in the war (World War Two). He knew Queen Victoria had named his area the Black Country and how the Quakers were instrumental in helping Birmingham become a city. Luckily his first piece of conversation about the zoo intrigued her mother. He was able to talk about catching a double decker bus to Dudley and how the semi-ruined castle was set on a hill overlooking Dudley. The zoo was in the castle grounds and he had seen many animals and they had impressed a young Charley.

He was relieved when Nur's father interrupted to say he wanted to look at precious stones. In the office Charley was confronted with a few fairly large stones. He gravitated immediately to a shiny ruby. This was a nice well cut stone with a deep colour but Charley thought he detected a flaw. He said for sure he would need a bright light behind the stone and the desk lamp was not bright enough. Nur's father became excited and asked how they could get such a light. Charley described a strong light behind a glass plate in a frame. They could use black paper to cover the glass and have a hole for the stone to sit in the light. Nur was smiling at Charley as her father was writing this down. Charley looked at a few more stones but was only really interested in the ruby.

The evening was a great success and Nur complimented Charley.

"Not only did you entertain my mother but you set my father a task. I could see the excitement in his face and I think the stones became secondary. Now I am going to work on my mother."

Back in the barracks he would sit quietly and contemplate his good luck. He wrote letters to his mother and his grandparents and told them after marriage he was going to live in Singapore. Of course, he was hoping he could get married to Nur; there was also the warm climate He would resign from the army and hoped he could have a job lined up before he was free. In the camp library he found a small book on gem stones and some had their chemical formulae. One of the troops knew some chemistry and so he enlisted his help in trying to understand the formulae. The soldier only had an elementary knowledge of chemistry but could identify the elements and work out the formulae.

After a few days Nur reported that her father had built the light set-up and had already given it a try. She said he was collecting more stones and wanted to make a night of viewing. Nur was surprised that her father was good with his hands. He told her before he became a merchant he used to build things and now he was enthusiastic to do that again. This was all news to Nur. She said her father was laughing more than normal and was even pleasant with her brothers. Her mother was happy and told Nur to bring Charley to their home again.

The evening was arranged and Charley had brushed up on the royal family. It turned out that was not necessary as after dinner they were whisked off to the office. Charley admired the light set-up and that brought smiles all around. The father tipped out quite a few stones but Charley immediately picked out the ruby which he examined from all angles. He finally said that there was a minor flaw possibly where two stones had grown together or one had come under stress. If the stone was being sold to an expert it might be found but otherwise to sell it as a perfect stone. Nur's father smiled.

The next stone he picked was a sapphire; he had seen many in the Jewellery Quarter. This was a beautiful stone well cut and without flaws. Charley explained that the ruby and the sapphire were mainly aluminium oxide and the colour was determined by the metal impurity. His audience was impressed. Although he admitted he had little idea of local prices he thought this stone should be expensive. Again the father was smiling and Nur was nodding approval.

Most of the other stones were smaller but there was one small emerald that was well cut and without a flaw. Charley told them this was aluminium silicate with the green colour coming from the metal impurity. Many of the remaining stones were zircons which he regarded as cheaper stones probably good for rings and necklaces. He divided up the stones into three piles according to his estimation of price.

"We have been educated and entertained, you may call me Aadam. I must thank you for setting me on a new tack, now I can go into the market with knowledge."

Charley said, "I am not sure how you sell your gems but I think you should make a cabinet to display the lesser stones such as the zircons. Often a display attracts people even they are not interested in the stones and they might buy on impulse."

Aadam said, "That is a wonderful idea. I will make a cabinet myself."

On their way to the barracks Nur said, "How do you do it? My dad is so happy and if he is happy so is my mom. I am now going to soften them up about the marriage."

"Soften them up sounds like one of my phrases, you are a quick learner. I think that is one of your qualities."

"One of my qualities is that I listen to everything you say; I will make a good wife."

Charley knew Nur would make a good wife but would he make a good husband? He received two letters from England; he opened his grandfather's letter first. He cautioned him on a mixed marriage but told Charley to do what he thought best. Why did he want to stay in Singapore was his grandfather's question? Charley thought of a foggy November night and there was the answer. His grandmother's part was less encouraging, she did not want him to live in a foreign country. Come back to England was her plea. For some reason Charley did not really think of Singapore as a foreign country.

He opened his mother's letter hoping for some encouragement. This was not to be the case, she was upset he was to marry a brown girl and he should come home and marry an English girl. She would not attend the wedding and she was hoping it would not occur. Her hope was that the army would transfer him to another place. Charley was not going to let that happen; he was definitely staying in Singapore. He reread the letter and became angry; he knew what he was doing and was going to do it.

He sat back with these letters and thought for a long time; they were not going to change his mind. His mother's very negative response hit him hard. He regretted not sending a photo of Nur with his letters but it might not have made any difference. These letters were not going to be shown to Nur; he even thought of tearing his mother's into small pieces. No matter, Singapore was going to be his home come what may. Now he had to think seriously about a job.

Nur said that her father wanted Charley to come to one of his shops to see the display cabinet. Charley went to the shop and met Nur's brother Joseph. Aadam greeted Charley and was proud to show his work. Charley said he liked it but it needed to stand alone not overwhelmed by other items. Aadam gave out a cry that

Charley did not understand and then he was being hugged. Nur explained that her father had praised God, he was so happy with the idea. Her father never hugged anyone. Jacob stood back and watched. He was then ordered to clear space for the cabinet. Jacob was congratulating his father on a very good case and he also shook hands with Charley. They all stood back and admired the display standing alone without clutter.

After leaving the shop Charley and Nur went to the café. Nur was kissing him and the Chinese owner was laughing and putting his thumbs-up. It looked like everyone was happy.

"My dad does not hug my brothers, he does not hug anyone. Now I will tell him we have to keep you in the company and I will marry you to make you stay."

"I don't think that will work but if it does you are a crafty bugger; oh sorry for swearing. I think you are picking up my sense of humour and I love it."

Nur gave him a big kiss; she loved his expressions and his humour. Charley had let her shed her inhibitions by showing her love in public. He had also allowed her father to shed his inhibitions by hugging Charley.

After a few days Nur reported that her father was willing to take on Charley and wanted to talk to him. She admitted she had not got around to talking about marriage. Now it was up to Charley; he had to prepare.

"Good afternoon, Aadam, I am here to talk to you about my future and have two topics. Firstly, I understand you could employ me when I resign from the army; that is welcome news. I think my understanding of accountancy and taxation law could be useful along with my expertise in jewellery."

Aadam was smiling and nodded in the affirmative.

"I know little about your business but I know you have two shops. Which is most profitable and how can we make them more profitable?"

"Very good question, they are not the same size so how could we compare them?"

"We need to look at the books and compare overheads such as rents, location and sales."

"Rents are no problem as I own both shops but what do I do if they are unequal?"

"You could first try swapping managers and also looking at the locations so you could assess passing trade."

"Every time I meet you I am set a problem. What is your next topic?"

"This topic is very personal; I would like to ask your permission to marry your daughter."

Aadam sat very quiet for a while that seemed like an age to Charley. Charley was trying not to fidget.

"I cannot give you an answer at present I must discuss it with Nur and my wife."

The meeting ended with a handshake and Charley was so glad to leave. This was a very new experience; Aden had been a cake walk compared with this encounter. Later when he met Nur he told her what had happened and she now had the problem. Another problem occurred to Charley, would he have to change religion? He decided to ask her about religion.

"We are Christians; I think we were converted in Malaya about three generations ago. My brothers are Joseph and Paul and my dad's name is our version of Adam. My name is a traditional name and my mom's name is Mary, it is actually Maryam. I hope and assume you are a Christian."

"Yes, I am nominally a Christian but a non-practising one. I haven't been to church since I was young. We had a church nearby but I hated Sunday school, they always wanted us to memorize passages in the Bible. How is the discussion of marriage going?"

"That could take a little time as my mother is the biggest opponent. There are some rumblings from the relatives but my brothers have been suspiciously silent."

"I have never talked to Paul and only a brief conversation with Joseph. Should I meet them? Maybe they are afraid of their inheritance? I don't intend to interfere with any family business."

"I will arrange a meeting, but I am going to be there."

The four met at the café and Paul was the first to speak.

"Why do you want to marry my sister?"

"Well, she is the most beautiful girl I have ever met and also the most intelligent. I understand she can cook but I have not sampled that yet. She understands everything I say and she speaks perfect English and she can teach me to speak properly."

"You know our father is rich. Does that have any motivation for this marriage?"

"Yes, I know your father is rich and I want to make him richer but Nur and I will make our way in this world without any inheritance. I understand male heirs always take precedence in this society. I have never owed any man money and I don't intend to in the future. By the way that last sentence includes your father, mother and any other of Nur's relatives."

Joseph spoke up. "Will you go back to England?"

"I want to stay in Singapore and the only attraction in England is my mother and grandparents. The climate in Singapore is much better for me than in England. The prospects for me are better here. In Singapore I am not seen as small and that appeals to me. I will try to show Nur England but I want to live here. I am sure Nur will enjoy a visit but it would be very difficult for her to live in England."

Paul asked, "Is that because of her colour?"

"No, that does not seem to matter these days, the difficulty would be the climate and to some extent the living conditions."

Nur was nodding approval with everything he said but did not say a word. After a few more questions they settled down to polite chatter and Nur joined in the conversation. Charley watched as she could dominate the conversation. Finally as they were leaving Paul said,

"My sister is father's favourite and I think you will win."

"Well, that was easier than I expected. I assumed your brothers would be aggressive. Their questions were easy and they were very friendly. I noticed when you joined the conversation they were not going to argue with you."

"The only aggressive ones in my family are my dad and mom and of course me and I am on your side. My brothers know that and did not want a family argument in front of you. I now find that all my suitors were proposed by my mother, my dad did not propose one. You are the one who can make both my dad and me happy, none of the others could do that. I am working on my dad as he will make the decision. If the worst comes to the worst, a phrase I learned from you, I will wait till I come of age."

After a week Aadam called for a meeting. Charley was surprised Nur's brothers were not present. After the dinner Aadam rose to speak.

"I have decided to give my consent to this marriage. There are a few conditions, the first being that Nur will first graduate from University. When she does she will be the first in our family. Charley will leave the army and will temporarily live in a flat above one of my shops. After marriage they will live in our house until I find suitable accommodation. The wedding will be in our church and I will pay for the reception. Charley's family will be invited to the wedding but I am afraid I will have to disappoint some of our large family. Have you any questions?"

Charley did not want to think of one and Nur was silent. Aadam continued to speak about Nur.

"Nur was about four-months-old when my mother first saw her. She told me this girl would be different and not to stand in her way. I did not understand at that time but every time I had problems with my daughter my mother was in my brain. I knew Nur would be different but I did not envisage how different. I now wonder what my mother would say and that is why I approve of this marriage. Normally I don't drink but I have an old bottle of brandy that we will use to congratulate the coming bride and groom. I hope they have a long and happy marriage."

Nur and her mother did not drink and that left Charley and Aadam to toast in brandy and the ladies to toast in water.

On their way back to the barracks Nur said she had never seen her father drink alcohol and never heard him talk of his mother. "You make my father say and do things I never expected."

"Well, that was the best brandy I have ever tasted I think it was an old brandy. I tried some Greek stuff in Cyprus but there is no comparison. What happens now?"

"Leave that to me. I will let you know."

Within days, Charley, as he called it, 'gave in his notice' and he was free. Nur reported that her father used to drink before he was married. She found out a bit more from her mom who was not happy about the marriage. Her dad had smiled when Nur was born and had rarely smiled since. Her dad seemed to love Nur more than her brothers and would never stand in her way. Charley was the only person who had made her dad excited in the last few years. Her mom was resigning herself to the marriage.

Charley left the barracks with lots of handshakes and when Nur collected him there were lots of wolf whistles. Nur smiled and gave them a thumbs-up, something she had learnt from Charley. There were a few phrases like 'lucky bugger' as they left. Charley was telling Nur to take no notice but they were really a nice bunch of men.

The flat where Charley was to stay (above the shop) was a bedsitter with a toilet and shower. There was a gas stove, a bed, a table and four chairs and little else, but there was a sink. There was no fridge and Nur said Charley could not live there.

"I have a bed, a stove to make tea and everything outside will provide me with any food I need. If I need company I go downstairs and serve in the shop. I think Aadam is giving me a test and I will show I can cope with any situation. This is the perfect place for me to learn more about Singapore. I will also learn about the shop and how things work."

The flat was above the shop run by the Chinese manager. Nur went off to university and Charley sat in the back of the shop watching the comings and goings. After a while when he got used to prices he asked the manager to sit in the background and he would try to sell. Customers were confused when they saw Charley behind the counter. He engaged them in conversation telling them he wanted to live in Singapore and so he had to sell to earn a living. After a few hours the manager relieved him and said some items had been sold for more than the asking price. Word got back to Aadam and according to his wife he was doing a jig.

The first night in the flat was a bit strange, this was the first time he had slept alone for many years. In the barracks there was also a snorer or someone having a bad dream. The area outside never slept and there were different noises all night. The bed was comfortable and in the morning he was woken by a knock at the door. He put on his shorts and opened the door. It was Nur with his breakfast. Charley adjusted his sight to the light and gave her a kiss; he was not expecting this very welcome surprise.

"I cooked this myself and I hope you enjoy it as my mother says I am trying too hard."

"You forgot my glass of milk."

"Is that what they serve babies in the army?"

"I think you have absorbed too much of my humour."

Charley enjoyed his breakfast with a cup of tea and of course a beautiful lady watching him eat. His bed was just behind him and he was tempted to grab Nur but he resisted the temptation. He was telling himself to have self-control and wait till they were married.

"Dad would like you to visit the markets and I will be a little distance behind. He is interested in the reactions when they realize you are not a tourist. I think he is enjoying having you around."

Charley wandered around the market and asked prices and picked up many trinkets. Many had a 'Made in Birmingham' sign and he would tell the stall holder that was where he was from. As he was buying nothing there were a few quizzical looks but they would not turn away a potential buyer. Nur would be a few feet away generally following but occasionally getting in front of Charley so as not to arouse suspicion; she loved her task. She had rarely been to a market.

She reported to her father that the stall holders were confused and did not know what to make of Charley. Nur was happy to do that again but she had to go to university the next day and could not follow Charley. Her heart was telling her to miss class but her brain was saying no.

"Why not ask your wife to follow me?"

Aadam frowned, nodded his head and then said, "Wait a minute."

When he had left Nur said, "I can't believe you said that."

"It was a spur of the moment decision but I have to get to know your mother. I thought what better than a stroll around a market with her trailing behind?

Thinking it over I am not sure whether it was the right thing to say."

Aadam came back all smiles. Maryam would love a tour of one of the markets. She is keen to see the changes

"My wife knew all the markets when we were young but nobody will know her now."

When they were alone Nur told Charley she could not believe what he was doing to her family. The thought of her mother trailing Charley through the markets would never have crossed her mind.

"My dad is smiling, my mother is going to follow you around the market, my brothers are silent and I cannot wait to see what happens next."

The next day Charley consulted Maryam. This was the first time he had talked to her alone. She decided which market to visit and the tactics to employ. She was dressed in rather drab clothes and just looked like an old grandmother out shopping. In the market she told Charley not to walk too fast. After they had finished their tour, Charley went back to his flat for a cold drink. That cold drink had to be a beer.

Later he met Nur who was in a very happy state. Her mom had loved the market, it had brought back memories. The sellers were confused about this little Englishman who spoke English in a funny way and looked at everything but bought nothing. In the market Charley reverted to his dialect and 'Made in Birmingham' was changed to 'Made in Brummagem' which was totally confusing to the locals. Maryam wanted to go to a different market the next day. Charley had planned to look at the books but he could not say no to his future mother-in-law. Nur told him that after their tour had finished her mother went back to the market to buy a few trinkets that she did not really need.

"Now my mother wants to go out more, you have lifted some kind of barrier and she is going to enjoy a new freedom. She wants my dad to take her out to a hotel with a good restaurant; she wants to dress up rather than dress down as in the market. My dad is normally in control but I think he is buckling. I am sure that word comes from you as so many things these days."

Charley was going to go out with his future in-laws, which was a new experience. He had a suit and two good shirts which had never been worn. Arthur had introduced him to an Indian tailor who had made a lightweight dress suit and two dress shirts; his problem was shoes. He had an old pair of shoes, his army boots and sandals which he was wearing all the time. The imported shoes were very expensive. Jacob directed him to a shoemaker and he had a simple pair of shoes made. He would have liked brogues but they would take too long to make. The shoes arrived on the afternoon before the dinner. He tried them thinking they would need breaking in but they were a perfect fit. Now he felt comfortable he would be dressed like a real gent and not out of place in a good hotel.

Dressed with his regimental tie he found he did not have a mirror but the Chinese shop manager found one so he could look at himself. The shop manager told him he looked very smart. He thought Aadam would approve. As Charley walked to Aadam's house he saw many people looking at him. They thought a white man in a suit should have been at Raffles and not walking in their local district.

Nur was smiling when she said, "You really look smart. I have never seen you dressed in a suit."

"You look wonderful in that dress, I normally see you in jeans but you look good in anything."

"Remember I am a student and jeans are what we wear. This is turning out to be a special event, dad has hired a chauffeur-driven car for the evening. I have never known him to do that. Mom has had her hair done and she is dressed in the most beautiful outfit I have ever seen. I don't know how long she has had the outfit but I have never seen her wear it."

Maryam entered the room and Charley said, "Maryam, you take my breath away. I would love the market people to see you now."

Maryam smiled and said, "Thank you but this is not for their eyes."

Aadam entered the room and was taken aback by the sight of his company; he said nothing but had a broad smile.

As they entered the hotel they met Paul and his manager. Aadam saw Paul first and interrupted Paul's conversation. Paul was surprised and speechless at first. Then he introduced his manager, Pierre. Aadam shook his hand and introduced Pierre to his wife. He stood back as Pierre spoke to his Maryam.

"Enchante, Madame, you have just made this hotel a special place." He then kissed her hand.

Pierre was introduced to Nur and Charley, her future husband.

"This hotel should invite you ladies to come here every night, you make the place shine."

He then kissed Nur's hand.

"If you are English you must be the luckiest Englishman in Singapore."

"Yes, I am English from Birmingham."

"I know it well. I visit the Jewellery Quarter quite often."

Charley would love to have carried on the conversation but the time and place was inappropriate. They said their good evenings and entered the restaurant. Aadam was in a good mood and had determined to have a drink. He ordered two large scotches and soft drinks for the ladies. Charley would have liked a beer but the scotch was good. The menu was very British with dishes such as roast beef and Yorkshire pudding, roast lamb with mint sauce and roast pork with apple sauce. Charley enjoyed his meal but was wondering whether the others enjoyed their dishes. All in all the dinner was a success and Charley did get a couple of beers. He enjoyed the ride home with Aadam saying they would do this again.

Meeting Pierre had given Charley a few ideas about collaboration with foreign companies. He was still taking his taxation course and he could use the university law library after graduation. He wanted to use the library to study company law particularly focusing on foreign collaboration. Now he had to investigate foreign companies operating in Singapore.

As they walked back to Charley's flat Nur was full of interesting observations. Her mother and father were a revelation; she had never seen either of them so relaxed. She had watched her father enjoying his scotch and water. Paul's reaction was interesting as he was so surprised to see his parents in an upmarket hotel. She had never eaten a real English meal and was not too keen. Charley agreed and said she should have put mustard on her roast beef as English meals were not very spicy.

The next time Charley was able to wear his suit was at Nur's graduation. He had a pair of brogues made and was very happy with them. He now felt comfortable in his suit even though he had to wear a tie. Nur looked so different in her cap and gown; he had rarely seen her head covered except with the occasional shawl. He thought she would use high heeled shoes but she said she was afraid of falling over when she collected her degree. Charley was glad as she would have towered over him in stilettos. Aadam was so proud he was beaming and Maryam had tears in her eyes. Nur was the first in her family to go to university and she was graduating with a first class degree in Economics. Paul and Jacob were there with some relatives Charley had never met. Charley was loving the pomp and ceremony and regretting that he was too old to go to university. He had left school at fifteen and picked up most of his knowledge since.

After the graduation there was a reception in a big hall. Nur was surrounded by fellow students and Charley had to remain in the background admiring his future wife. One of Nur's lecturers came to talk to Charley. He wondered whether Charley would give a lecture about his early life. This man was giving lectures in international studies and said his students had no idea how other people lived. Charley was a bit reluctant and then Aadam stepped in and urged him to say yes. Charley could hardly refuse his boss so he agreed, after all he told much of his story to students in the café; the only difference was that he would have to put his stories in some sort of order and would leave out his leaving school at fifteen.

Finally Nur extracted herself from the well-wishers and came over to give Charley a big kiss. Charley was a bit embarrassed but Nur told him not to worry as her friends knew she was different and her parents were in a happy state. She knew most of her friends would make conventional marriages and have ordinary lives but she wished a few would break out of the mould. Charley was thinking of Nur as an adventurer.

After the reception they went to a hotel, this one had a Chinese restaurant more suited to the company. Aadam was in a very generous mood and anyone who wanted a drink could have a couple, as he had arranged for taxis to take them home. He gave a couple of speeches and the second one after a couple of scotches was the most entertaining. He talked about his early married life and having children while trying to make his fortune. Maryam did not seem to mind and she was enjoying herself, she was laughing and surprising her sons. Paul drank but Jacob did not, the Chinese shop manager also enjoyed a drink. Charley watched Paul and Jacob as their dad was speaking. Jacob was enjoying it but Paul was frowning.

Charley was writing letters to his mother, his grandparents, Trevor in Hong Kong and Arthur in London. He included a photo of Nur's graduation in the letter to his mother. He was hoping she would change her mind and she would come to the wedding. The reply indicated she was not budging in her refusal to come to Singapore. Trevor loved Hong Kong and had just married a Chinese girl. In Trevor's letter there was a proposal to visit Singapore one day en route to England. His wife Li wanted to see England. Charley thought it might be good to go together to England. Arthur was trying to set up a tailoring business in south London. He had found a shop and already had some customers. He was missing warm Singapore and wished he could have stayed but in London he was going to make his 'fortune'.

Charley received his diploma in taxation law and Nur was very proud of him; he was the only white student in the class. One privilege of his diploma was that he had a pass to use the university facilities. Nur treated him to a dinner in an Indian restaurant; they both enjoyed Indian food. Charley told her Indian food was becoming popular in England and she said she could not wait to try English/Indian food. Charley's tailor was part owner of the restaurant and he was able to get a good deal. He was making all sorts of contacts in Singapore and occasionally they were useful.

The stocktaking and reconciliation of the accounts showed that the Chinese-run shop was doing better than the one run by Jacob. Aadam had no problem with relocating the shop managers. Charley thought that Jacob might be upset but talking to him he realised that his father was the ruler. Actually, Charley liked to chat with Jacob and he was learning things about the family that maybe Nur would not tell him.

The wedding was imminent and Charley had asked whether Nur would like to spend a week in Malaya in the area he had loved, this would be a local honeymoon. They would spend the first night at home and then travel by train to the north. He suggested they stay at one of the clubs and have a peaceful time. Nur was very keen. She had never been out of Singapore and having a peaceful time with Charley sounded like bliss. She was also excited about going on a train. A quiet time was planned but then there were relatives in the area. Charley also promised they would have a second honeymoon in England when they could afford it. Nur was kissing Charley and said two honeymoons would be good but how about more. Now that set Charley thinking; maybe Africa or Cyprus.

Charley went to the barracks and sought out some of the troop he still knew. He asked one bloke if he would be best man. He also invited seven others to the church and reception. He told them to stay sober and keep it in their trousers. They all liked Charley and promised to be on their best behaviour. He then went to have a chat with the priest (Simon) who turned out to have a Malay mother and an English father from Coventry. His father had died when Simon was young and he was brought up by the church. Simon never found out what killed his father and there was no death certificate. His mother could not cope and as a good Christian had given him to the priest. The priest's wife took care of Simon and of course he attended church every day and went to the church school. His English was very good but he had no Coventry accent. This church was well endowed and Simon was never hungry. Simon asked about religion in England and Charley admitted he was not really a practising Christian; this did not upset Simon.

Charley had a tour of the church which was beautiful. The stained glass windows were impressive and this looked like a rich church. Simon explained that he would ask who gave the bride and also who gave the groom. In many cases there would be an arranged marriage and so both families were involved. Some of these arrangements started almost from birth. Families were very involved in the marriage and the future life of the couple; sometimes families were too involved. Charley knew his boss would be very involved with his marriage but he did not mind.

Charley sensed Nur was getting nervous and so he told her it was a walk in the park. That one slipped over her head and she asked which park? He said he was only joking and all brides got nervous. He told her about the priest and she was surprised he had not taken her with him.

"I know little or nothing about your church so I had to familiarize myself before we met the priest together. I also wanted to see the church, which by the way is beautiful. The priest is a very nice fellow and I learnt a lot talking to him. We discussed the service which was all new to me. He told me about his history and the history of the church. The Japanese occupation was a hard time for the church but they came through it and now he generally had a large congregation; the church was doing well."

Charley was also getting nervous about the wedding. He had written again to his mother but she would not come. Arthur and Trevor were wishing him luck and a happy letter from granddad picked up his spirits. He wished his grandfather could come to Singapore. The market people were now recognizing him but they were still friendly. In the evening when he did not see Nur he would sit outside the shop and watch the comings and goings. He enjoyed a couple of cold beers and was happy with the sights. This hustle and bustle was so different to looking at the rubber plantation. If he could get a job in the rubber plantation country he would love to live there but he was stuck living in the city.

Charley and Nur went to see the priest together to discuss the ceremony. The meeting was very informal and although Nur had seen the priest before she had never spoken to him. Charley and Simon chatted like old friends and that pleased Nur. They went through the service and what was expected of the bride and groom; Simon said there would be no problem unless someone objected. After leaving the church Nur said she enjoyed the last thirty minutes and they should make friends with Simon. Charley agreed as long as they did not have to go to church too often.

Charley had a wedding suit made and his brogues suited very well. He picked his best man and he was in full uniform; Charley wished he could have worn his uniform with the corporal stripes. His best man was watching as Nur entered on her father's arm and said WOW! Charley was almost afraid to look. When he looked all he could see was a white blur, then he started to sweat. Nur stood beside him and she seemed much taller, luckily she was not wearing high heels. Through her mask she said, "I ope youm awright" using her best Birmingham accent. Charley wanted to laugh but he relaxed and decided not to reply.

The priest looked at Charley and winked and now Charley was really relaxed. The ceremony proceeded and the priest asked who would give the bride and Aadam was very loud in his reply. When the priest asked who would give the groom, seven soldiers rose and in unison said, "We do." There was a hush and the priest said, "I assume no one has an objection."

Charley was so relieved no one objected and also the soldiers had behaved themselves. At the reception all the soldiers had drunk in moderation. Even Aadam said that they must have respect for Charley. Aadam was very happy with the bridal service and told Simon to expect a large donation. Maryam quietly cried throughout the service and curtseyed to Simon. Nur was holding Charley tightly at every opportunity. She was even holding him when he was being greeted by her brothers. Paul remarked that he had never seen his sister so possessive. Jacob was laughing and shaking Charley's hand vigorously. Charley danced with Nur and it was the first time their bodies had been pressed together, in public that is. Actually Charley was happy when the reception was over as he was getting tired.

During the reception a man approached Charley who said, "She will not make a good housewife, too educated."

Charley replied "I don't want a good housewife."

The man disappeared and Charley turned to Nur. "Who was that?"

"He is a cousin on my mother's side. Dad did not want to invite him as he is a drunkard and a gambler. We see him now and again when he wants money, dad will give him nothing but I think mom does."

Charley watched Paul and Jacob. Paul did not look happy but Jacob was smiling and laughing. Charley thought he should have a chat with Paul in the future and find out the problem. Charley could not wait to leave the reception and was glad to get in the limousine to take them home.

They were now home in Nur's bedroom standing looking at each other. Nur had ridden herself of her wedding dress but Charley was fully dressed. Nur asked whether she should help him take off his suit. Charley could only stare at his bride but that comment jerked him into action. All the while he was divesting himself of his clothes he could not take his eyes off his wife. Finally they were both naked looking at each other. This was the first in the flesh nude woman he had seen. Soldiers always had magazines but this was real.

"I think Percy is ready."

"Who is Percy?"

Charley pointed to his erect penis.

"Let's see if he can do a good job."

With that Nur jumped on the bed to be followed by Charley. After a bit of fumbling Percy was inside and then Charley found he was on his back. Nur was doing all the work saying, "I have waited a long time for this." She kept up her vibrations even after Charley had climaxed. Finally she gave a sigh and stopped. As she rolled off Charley he said, "I think we forgot foreplay."

"We can leave that till next time."

As he lay next to Nur he could not believe his luck, that was all so easy and the banter had reduced his nerves. She was so beautiful and her skin so soft and brown. His mother was right, he had married a brown-skinned girl who was really out of his league. He was wondering if he should ask her what she saw in him but he decided that could wait. At this moment Charley thought nothing could be better than this.

In the morning they both showered and Nur suggested they shower together but somehow Charley resisted that temptation. After his shower Nur presented him with her luggage, one small suitcase. He frowned and looked for another bag. There was none.

"I thought all women tried to fill at least two suitcases."

"I am a different woman, we are going to the country and I assume there will be no ball. I have what I think I need."

"Well, I have my new safari suit but I am not sure about the safari." They both laughed and kissed.

After breakfast they walked to Charley's former flat above the shop and collected his suitcase. He had bought a local case as he only had a back pack. Since leaving the army Charley had acquired a lot of things, mainly clothes. Reaching the train station Nur was excited, she had never been on a train. Charley found she had been to very few places even on the island. She had never been into Malaya, no wonder she lapped up his stories about Cyprus, Aden and Kenya.

Nur was enjoying the train ride and was reluctant to get off. She negotiated with the taxi driver to get to their destination; she had never negotiated before. They reached the club and booked in while Charley showed their marriage certificate, which was not necessary. Charley did not want any false assumptions. The certificate was a church document and the civil document would be available on their return. They unpacked their meagre belongings while Charley was being continually kissed. Lunch was a beer, a sandwich and a Chapman's. Nur liked the taste of the Angostura bitters. They sat on the balcony admiring the scenery, rows and rows of trees. Nur was trying to follow the flights of the birds and listening to their sounds. She admitted that in the city she never noticed the birds and she had never seen so many trees in orderly lines.

Everything was so peaceful and Charley was telling Nur to relax and enjoy the peace. It was broken by the approach of a fairly tall man.

"Hello, I am your uncle Joshua."

"I thought I recognized you, you are my father's youngest brother. This is my husband, Charley."

"Pleased to meet you, sir. I have heard a lot about you."

"Pleased to meet you, sir. I hope most of it was good."

"When I was told my brother was letting his daughter marry an Englishman I realised you must be something special. Now I am thinking my brother is more progressive than me. I am sorry I could not get to your wedding but when I knew you were in the district I arranged a small reception for you tonight. A car will pick you up at five p.m. Now I must do a little business in the club."

"Are you a member, sir?"

"Yes, I am one of the patrons, I like this club and come for some peace and quiet. I see you are enjoying the scenery, very different from the city but much quieter."

Charley was thinking Joshua must be a big man in the district. He was a patron of the club so he must have some influence in the area. Charley was thinking so much for a candlelit dinner but a party is a party. Nur was explaining to Charley that she could not say no to her uncle. Charley was perfectly at ease going to a small reception. Then Nur's next problem was how to dress. Charley thought her simple dress was more suitable than jeans. She agreed and kept kissing him. She wondered how her uncle had tracked them down but a phone call from her father had probably been all that was needed. Later she found that Jacob had made the call.

They were sitting on the front porch at five p.m. when one of the waiters told them a car was waiting; the car turned out to be a Rolls-Royce. Charley had never ridden in a Rolls-Royce and has enchanted by the interior. He spied a drinks cabinet but was not game to open it. The reception was anything but small, there was Joshua's family and lots of distant relatives. There were friends including a British rubber plantation manager Charley had met before while on patrol. As Joshua introduced the guests he asked Nur to speak English. That was not necessary for Charley. Joshua explained he wanted them all to learn English and he was keen on his sons and daughters going to university. The ladies were all well dressed with lots of jewellery and make-up. Nur soon forgot her self-consciousness as all the women were admiring her dress. Joshua loved the English expression *breath of fresh air* and he said Nur was certainly that. He was watching the ladies and only a couple were frowning, most were smiling. Joshua was very happy Nur had come simply dressed, again it was a breath of fresh air. Joshua's children were loving Nur She was not used to .small children but was smiling all the time.

Charley gravitated to the plantation manager and they engaged in discussion. Charley was just glad to be with someone he knew. The manager told him Joshua was a big man in the area. Charley had gathered that at their meeting and looking at the guests it reinforced his view.

"You have married a very different Malay woman, I should know as I have known many Malay women. Your wife has the kind of dress I might see in a summer in England. She appears to have no jewellery or make-up and I can't find fault with her English."

Charley said, "She only packed one dress as we were not expecting a reception. She does not like or wear jewellery and her beauty means there is no need for make-up. My wife is a university graduate and I am teaching her how to become a Brummie."

"Then on that last count she has my sympathy."

They both laughed at that last remark. Joshua saw they were enjoying each other and came to join them.

"I have plenty of whisky and brandy if you like."

"Thank you, sir, but in this climate I like cold beer although your brother likes whisky."

"You mean Aadam drinks whisky, that is news to me. I must visit him and take him a good bottle. I will have a car at your disposal if you wish to see a little more of the countryside."

The plantation manager said, "I have an idea, the day after next I have what I call a cutter coming to the plantation to get rubber from some as yet untouched trees. This man is an expert and a pleasure to watch."

"I would love to see him work and I am sure Nur would love the experience. I am enchanted with these plantations."

When the reception was over they were taken back to the club and Charley told Nur of the planned trip to the plantation. She could not wait but first she could not wait for bed. The next day was a quiet day with a long walk, lots of quiet time on the balcony and a candle-lit dinner. Charley asked Nur whether she was bored but she said she loved every minute. She had lots of practice using Malay with passers-by and she said she was learning all the time. Charley was getting worried his condom supply would not last the week.

Early next day they were picked up and taken to the plantation. The manager introduced the 'cutter' and his mate. Nur had a long discussion with him before they set out. He had explained what would happen but they should stand back as his knife was very sharp. They watched as he made four strokes and peeled back the bark. He then stuck a straw-like object in the tree at the bottom of one of his cuts. Then he positioned a bucket below this spout and moved to the next tree. The whole procedure was over in less than two minutes. Nur could not believe the speed of the operation. The manager explained this was probably the best 'cutter' in the district. His mate had a wheel barrow with buckets and he would return to get more as the supply was depleted.

After a while they retired to the manager's office for a cold drink. The cutter would do more trees before he took a drink. Nur could not stop talking about the skill and speed of the cutter. The manager explained that mechanization was coming and the cutters' days were numbered. Nur wanted to go outside to watch the cutter. While Charley had a private time with the manager he asked where he could get condoms. The manager reached into his desk and gave Charley six condoms with a big grin.

The rest of the week passed peacefully but all Nur could talk about was the cutter. On the evening before they were leaving for Singapore Joshua came to dinner. He was very happy, all his children wanted to be like 'aunty' Nur. He did not remind them she was their cousin. Nur and Charley were the first mixed race couple they had met and he was telling them that was the future. Joshua was still intrigued with his eldest brother drinking whisky. Charley told him about going to the market with Maryam and Joshua was astonished. He told Nur her husband must be a wizard; he could never envisage Maryam going to the market with a white man.

Back in Singapore Nur had many stories for her parents. She loved Uncle Joshua and Aadam was very happy. Her father was very interested in the cutter and said when he was a boy he watched men working in the rubber plantations. Aadam reminisced about his childhood and this was mostly new to Nur. Her father had rarely talked about his childhood. Aadam was planning to go to Malaya when he had the chance.

Nur was now looking for a job and Charley was immersed in Aadam's finances. Aadam owned a four-storey block of flats. The top floor was occupied by the family of a friend and was really two flats. This friend was building a house and it was finished. Aadam decided that Nur and Charley would occupy one flat and they would refurbish the other for short term lets. Now Nur took charge and decided how she would decorate the second flat, Aadam was very glad to let her take charge, he knew she had his genes. He was smiling when Nur told him her plans.

The Chinese manager proved to be much better than Jacob and Charley wanted to help Jacob. He decided to put adverts outside the shop in English, he also put signs in the window in English. He told Jacob to talk to customers in English and if they were English to tell them his brother-in-law was from Birmingham. "Try not to sell them anything, let the customer make the choice."

Within a few days sales were up and Aadam was very pleased. He realised Jacob was the weaker of his sons and Nur was the much stronger than both. He knew Charley was a good influence on Jacob and he encouraged their interaction. Maryam was keen for more trips to the market but Charley was being recognized more often after his wedding. They still went to a market on the edge of town and Maryam bought some things she did not really need. Maryam was very happy and if she was happy Aadam was happy.

Charley was writing plenty of letters. In letters to his mom and grandparents he had enclosed photos of the wedding. His grandfather was very pleased with what he called a 'top class' wedding. His mother was less committal although she said she liked the photos. Arthur's letter was full of congratulations. He had set up a tailor's shop and had met a girl who he knew before joining the army. The disturbing reply was from Trevor who had been accused of stealing from the mess. There was going to be a court-martial although there was no evidence except missing money. Charley knew his friend was in charge of the mess and would never steal money from it. He was very sorry it was all going wrong for him.

A few months passed and Nur had a job with a shipping company. That started Charley thinking again about an export-import company. Aadam was keen but asked what could they export. Charley was looking around and the rubber industry was captured by big business. In the market there were a lot of knick-knacks, many from Birmingham. Souvenirs from Singapore took hold in his thoughts and then he came upon some jade carvings. He found a Chinese carver who was selling some of his wares to a few big hotels and chatted with him. He took Nur along as she could speak Cantonese. It was obvious the carver was being underpaid but Charley had to find a buyer in England or Europe.

In the meantime Trevor had written that he was going to England and would pass through Singapore. Nur was very keen to meet Trevor and his wife and they could stay for two weeks in the adjacent flat so they could iron out any problems. Aadam was happy as he was going to sign over the flats to his daughter; she would own them outright.

Aadam was also happy that his brother Joshua was going to visit. It had been a long time since he had seen his younger brother. Charley was going to talk to Joshua about hard wood; he knew Joshua had lots of influence in Malaya. The carver had told him that he liked to carve in wood but he preferred really hard wood.

Joshua arrived with a bottle of expensive single malt scotch for his brother. Joshua was full of praise for Nur and Charley. His sons and daughters were always talking about aunty Nur and uncle Charley. They were all going to do well in school and would go to university; little did they know that Charley left school at fifteen. Joshua thought an export-import company was a very good idea; he had access to various Malayan hard woods. He was also interested in the export business. Joshua sat down with his brother and found he was full of praise for Charley and was glad he had let Nur marry him. Joshua agreed and said Charley made a good impression wherever he went and had changed Aadam's family.

Joshua met Jacob who was pleased with his brother-in-law who always had good ideas. Charley was also a buffer between him and his father. Joshua roared with laughter at that comment.

Charley was now preoccupied with Trevor's arrival. Nur was very excited; she was going to meet another soldier's wife. Charley had told her of the times with Trevor. Trevor had introduced him to the café where they first met; in a sense Trevor had introduced Charley to Nur. Nur loved her thoughts about that café; it was only by chance she had gone there to meet Charley.

At the airport they all met and shook hands. As soon as Nur met the couple she knew Li Lin was going to be a friend. Nur had pointed out some time ago that she did not have many girl friends. Nur could use her Cantonese and English with this lady. Nur was fascinated with Li's story, walking from Canton to Hong Kong and being brought up in a church. Li had struggled to make a living and finally she and her sister had a tailoring business. This was all so different from Nur's life and she could not get over the hardship.

Li and Trevor were going to England to start a new life. Li was interested in fashion which was not at the forefront of Nur's thoughts. The way Li described the changes in clothing raised Nur's interest. In the market Li found her Cantonese useful and Nur could use her Malay to advantage. Nur suddenly found shopping with Li enjoyable. Charley and Trevor were visiting old haunts including some of the hotels. When Trevor was stationed in Singapore he was a sergeant and several of the posh hotels had refused him entry as they had a policy of 'officers only'. Now as a civilian he had no problem. Charley was well known as he frequented many hotels in a quest for partners in business.

The time passed quickly and Nur and Charley were unhappy to see Trevor and Li leave for England. They had enjoyed two weeks in their company. Nur told Charley she would miss Li but was jealous she was going to England.

Charley now started in earnest to try to find a way to open an export-import company. A good lead came from an unexpected source. In her work in shipping Nur encountered an Italian clearing agent who had a brother in Milan involved in importation. He might be interested in jade and wood carvings from Singapore. He was dealing with souvenirs and souvenirs from Singapore were unusual. Charley had the carver make one jade figure of a bird and a wood carving of a lion's head. The carver's son carved a bird in hardwood; actually Charley liked the boy's carving the best. Charley paid above the price being paid by the hotels. The carvings were sent by the clearing agent to his brother. Charley sat back and waited.

In the meantime he had a disturbing letter from Arthur who wanted to come to Singapore to escape the local press. He had been dating this girl who he knew before he was conscripted. On their third date he was with her in a restaurant when the police came and arrested her. She was part of a prostitution ring and they also arrested Arthur thinking he was her pimp. They both convinced the police that he was innocent but the local papers had hold of the story. He was being hounded by local journalists. Arthur had closed his shop and after fulfilling his orders was on his way to Singapore to escape the local newshounds. He was hoping Charley could help him hide and thought Singapore was a good place.

Charley met Arthur at the airport and found his friend in an agitated state. Some journalist had followed him to the airport but he thought he had lost him in departures. Charley calmed him and said he would stay in the apartment above the shop. Anyone trying to trace him would investigate the hotel guests. His new residence was not salubrious but no one would look for him in a room above a shop. They went to Charley's flat and Arthur received a cold beer to calm his nerves. As he relaxed he started to admire the view and then he was his old self. Charley said that after a short while he would introduce him to his Indian tailor. Nur was very happy to have another friend of Charley visiting Singapore. Charley did not tell her the full story. Jacob also liked having Arthur above the shop. He confided in Arthur that Charley was the best thing that had happened to his family.

The news from Milan was all good. The carvings had been exhibited in the shop window and there were several orders. Now Charley set Aadam thinking about what they could import from Italy. Charley supplied the carver with jade and hardwood and said to carve whatever he wished; he would get good money and not need to supply the hotels unless he wanted to keep them happy. Charley was keen to have the carver's son involved and so he took Nur along to fix the conditions. Nur loved to be involved and Charley was regularly rewarded.

News from England was not too good, Trevor could not find a job. He was also not enjoying living with his father. Charley could hardly remember living with his father but another letter from his mother gave some news about him. His mother was in touch with his auntie Ann who was his father's sister. She had said that his father had visited Singapore and had seen Charley but did not introduce himself; he was still travelling incognito. Charley was glad he had not met his father because he was not sure what he would have said. He then started wondering whether he would have recognized him; it had been a long time since he had seen him.

Arthur was enjoying his solitary life; his recent experience had shocked him. Jacob was his regular companion and he was enjoying the company. He was doing some work with the Indian tailor and working out some financial arrangements. The tailor was keen to use an English tailor in his advertisements; Arthur wanted to be called Archibald. Nur finally heard the full story and she was astounded that such a thing could happen in England. Charley started to think he had been painting too pretty a picture of his homeland. He realised he would have to show her England when he could afford the trip.

Trevor and Li were going back to Hong Kong via Singapore; England had been a disaster. Charley and Nur discussed where Trevor and Li would stay. The second apartment had been rented to a French family but Nur said their apartment had two bedrooms and Trevor and Li could stay with them. Trevor and Li had a very welcome greeting at the airport and Arthur was also persuaded to come. Nur and Li were so happy to see each other and Li had plenty of stories. Trevor, Charley and Arthur watched these two ladies embracing each other as though they were long-lost friends.

Trevor explained to his mates that his dishonourable discharge was the reason he could not find a job in England. He had been offered jobs in security but he wanted to be an accountant. His father was not sympathetic and Trevor felt they were interfering with his life. Li had a job in a Chinese restaurant and loved it but he could not wait to get back to Hong Kong. Arthur said that England had been a disappointment for both of them. Li was very upset with the weather as it was cold and rained almost every day.

Li and Nur had a lot to discuss, life in England, fashion and Trevor's father. Birmingham was a very big city and Li had found a job in a restaurant. The owner was Chinese and liked that she could speak English and Cantonese. Most of the Chinese staff had little English and she was a go-between the Chinese and English staff.

Some of the customers were very rude although most liked her English. Trevor's father was used to living alone and she tried to smooth arguments between Trevor and his father. England was cold and yet girls were out in miniskirts. Some were so short you could see their pants as they walked and worse when they bent over. Li had some sketches of the clothing and Nur was taken with them. She asked if she could have one. Li's description of Carnaby Street and the Kings Road market had Nur in another world; she had to see these places. Li liked riding on double decker buses and siting by a warm fire. She had never experienced a coal fire and went into great detail about how to light a fire.

Charley was telling Trevor that when he got back to Hong Kong he should work with the Chinese and forget the British companies. He should set up his own company and forget the past. Arthur was in agreement, he wanted to forget the past. Trevor said the thing that surprised him was that Li had invited his father to Hong Kong; secretly he was hoping his father would forget the invitation. Charley had nothing but praise for his in-laws, they had made his life in Singapore so easy. His father-in-law was a smart trader always open to new ideas.

Maryam invited Nur and Li to visit some markets with her. Nur was telling Li her mother had become liberated since she had been watching Charley in the market. Li became teary eyed as she told Nur about her mother. Maryam loved mixing Malay, Cantonese and

English while being escorted by two young ladies. She bought Li a rather expensive pearl necklace and Nur a silk scarf. Aadam invited everyone to a restaurant in an expensive hotel and he was so pleased with this company. There was plenty of whisky and beer for the men and Maryam tried a white wine although Li and Nur only drank Chapmans. Jacob was present but Paul was absent and Charley noted his absence.

With much hugging and kissing Trevor and Li left for Hong Kong and life settled back to normal. Charley had promised Nur they would visit uncle Joshua but all Nur could talk about was going to England. She suggested they could borrow money from her father but Charley did not like borrowing money he owed 'no man any money'. He was not keen on Nur's brother's reaction of his borrowing money from his father-in-law. The trade with Milan was going well and Aadam was in contact with their buyer. This man had suggested that the word Singapore should be somewhere in the carvings. Charley had talked to the carver's son and he was very enthusiastic about it. These carvings were three dimensional and Singapore was almost secreted into the carving. Their Italian client was ecstatic; he had a large store talking to him aboutthesecarvings. Jacob and Arthur were now becoming great friends. Jacob explained that in the family they did not discuss family matters with outsiders. He felt that had now been relaxed with Charley part of the family. Paul was the eldest and had been a bully when Jacob was young.

When Nur came along the family changed. His father seemed to be harder on the boys but very soft on Nur. Paul could not fight against his father but decided to get out by working for a foreign company. Jacob knew that Paul would inherit but he knew his father had planned something for them all. Now he had met his uncle he was going to work in Malaya. His uncle had seen the signs in English and was praising Jacob and offering him a job. Jacob did not tell his uncle the signs were Charley's idea. Jacob could only praise Charley but asked Arthur not to say anything about the conversation.

Charley was keen to go to Birmingham but he wanted enough money so he did not have to borrow. Even Joshua had offered to lend him money. The hardwood business had taken off and Joshua had a group of carvers. He had found an American buyer and wanted to cut Charley in on the profits. Charley had a plan that could cost him plenty. He planned to fly to Amsterdam and then go to Antwerp. He had written to Jacob and the reply had come that he was very welcome. They would fly to Birmingham and visit his mother and grandparents. Nur was insistent they visit London and particularly Carnaby Street.

After Charley had enough money he booked their flight. This was Nur's first flight and she was gripping Charley so tight the stewardess told her he could not escape. The immigration at Amsterdam looked at Nur's passport with suspicion and so Charley produced their marriage certificate. The immigration officers had a good laugh at this little Englishman having a beautiful Asian wife. They caught a bus to Antwerp and Nur was interested in the passengers who seemed to be talking many languages. Charley explained she could be hearing French, Dutch or Flemish and he could not tell her which. Charley had left most of their luggage in the airport but looking at the lady passengers he told Nur she might need some warm clothing.

Arriving in Antwerp bus station took Charley back many years. He stood and breathed deeply; Nur looked at him and asked if there was a problem. He explained his first smell of Europe and he was trying to remember the sensation. Charley explained his first trip and how he was almost lost. They took a taxi to Jacob's workshop and Nur was confronted by a seedy looking building. Charley explained that this Jacob was a diamond merchant and he and his workers cut diamonds. Inside, she would see things not many people ever would.

Jacob welcomed them and asked them to come to his office and sit at his desk. Nur looked around and saw a clean place very different to the building exterior. Jacob then pulled out a diamond, the biggest stone Nur had ever seen. Charley took a spy glass and said it was a very well cut stone but out of his price range. Jacob sat back in his chair with a big grin as Charley explained to Nur the cutting of the stone. Jacob reached into his pocket and produced an uncut stone. With his index finger he pointed to each stone without saying anything.

Suddenly the penny dropped and Charley realised this was the pair of uncut stones he had first seen. Jacob was laughing as he said this was Charley's stone. Charley said he could not afford such a stone. He had come to get a much smaller one which he could afford.

"My dear son, this is your stone as a wedding present. I have worked on it and it has not touched any other hand. Now we will go to my house for a celebration."

Nur watched all this in amazement, even Charley was shocked. She put on a scarf as she was introduced to all the women of the household. They all had their heads covered. Jacob's son was there shaking Charley's hand very vigorously, telling Charley his father was laughing again. Jacob's wife was explaining to Nur that Charley was like a son; Nur had a tear in her eye. Her husband was treated like royalty and she was there enjoying his treatment. Jacob made a speech in which he welcomed Charley and his new bride. He hoped they would have many children. Nur now started to think about children, after this journey it was something she desired.

Back at the hotel Charley said this was a much bigger diamond than he had planned and it was a very expensive wedding present. He would get it made into an engagement ring; she would have the best diamond in Singapore. Charley said, "Let's go to dinner and celebrate."

Nur was interested in the food in the hotel restaurant, there were many dishes she had never seen before. She decided to take pot luck, a phrase Charley had taught her. The soup contained lots of vegetables and was quite spicy. The main dish turned out to be smoked eel with vegetables. She loved both dishes. Charley had chicken soup followed by beef on a skewer with well-done chips. Nur had to pinch one or two of his chips which she also loved. Charley persuaded her to have a glass of sweet wine to toast their new acquisition; she liked the taste but felt it was going to her head. Charley said they should try the bed in Belgium and she agreed.

The next day they took the bus to Amsterdam to catch the flight to Birmingham. They were greeted at Birmingham airport; Charley was looking for Elmdon. He thought his mother's greeting was a bit reserved but his grandfather held nothing back. Charley had booked a hotel on the Hagley Road and everyone was invited to dinner. Charley had arranged for a taxi to take his guests home after a good meal and a few drinks. He was upset that his mother was a bit cold but Nur told him that when people meet they do not always enjoy the experience. Charley was thinking about enjoying the experience, it was so un-Birmingham. His grandfather's greeting was what he would expect from a Brummie.

After the guests had gone home Nur wanted to discuss the diamond. The plan was to make an engagement ring but Nur thought it would be too large for her finger. She liked her current (rather understated) ring and maybe the diamond was so special it should only be worn on special occasions. She proposed a necklace that she could wear at a party or a wedding. Charley could see the sense in the argument and he was not willing to argue with her.

The next day they caught a double decker bus to the Jewellery Quarter. Nur was excited about the bus and fascinated with the conductor who seemed to talk throughout the whole journey. When they got off she gripped Charley's arm, she had the diamond in her handbag. As they entered the workshop they were greeted by handshakes and one wolf whistle. The owner ushered them into his office and ordered tea. Charley had a long story to tell but he wanted to get down to business. Nur extracted the diamond from her bag and there were gasps from the workers. Several of the senior jewellers took a close look and they were all impressed. They generally agreed that a ring with that size stone could be a problem. The jeweller who normally specialized in necklaces sketched how the end product might look. Nur was impressed; the sketch reminded her of Li. As this piece was not going to be worn on a regular basis Charley suggested fourteen or eighteen carat gold. The owner smiled and said Charley had not lost the knowledge he gained in this building.

Lunchtime down the pub with the jewellers was a delight for Nur. She loved the atmosphere and was greeted by the publican and his wife. She studied the bar and the publican's wife explained how everything worked. She was relaxed the diamond was in the safe and the discussion was all about jewellery. The boss explained that Jacob had stopped coming from Antwerp but there were other family members who visited. They always had well cut diamonds to sell.

After lunch Charley decided to show Nur the centre of Birmingham. They caught a bus and wandered down to the Bull Ring market. He thought he should buy her something but he could not decide what. Nur spied nylon stockings and she wanted a pair, there were also some fancy stockings so she had two pairs and she told Charley that was enough. She knew she may never wear them in Singapore but she would show them to her mom. Charley walked her to the Town Hall and she was fascinated by the buildings. She was also watching the traffic, it was so orderly.

Charley now had a few days to see England and he asked Nur where she wanted to go and the answer was Carnaby Street. Li had told Nur to visit at the weekend when some of the more outrageous people were around. Charley booked a hotel in London for Saturday and Sunday nights. They would catch the train early on the Saturday morning and return on Monday morning. Nur was impressed with Snow Hill station and the cleanliness of the trains.

They arrived before noon and had lunch in a pub. Nur was comparing this pub with the one in the Jewellery Quarter. Saturday afternoon in Carnaby Street was a revelation for Charley, he had never seen so many pretty girls in skirts so short you could see their knickers. Men in flowered trousers had him shaking his head (a negative shake). Nur was fascinated by knee-length boots worn by the women and pointed shoes worn by the men. They looked in many shops and Charley was shaking his head. He was glad he was going to live in Singapore. Nur was explaining that Li had told her about these sights and now seeing was believing.

Besides Carnaby Street, Soho was an interesting area and they spent a few hours walking around the streets. Charley was seeing this area for the first time and could not explain some things to Nur. There seemed to be so many foreign restaurants. That weekend they got to see most of the sights including Buckingham Palace, Tower Bridge and the Tower of London. Charley thought that army life was good preparation for all this walking. Poor Nur was glad to get on the train to go back to Birmingham. She said she had enjoyed London except for the walking. She had seen what Li had told her about and would write Li a letter when she arrived home. The only problem was that England was so cold.

Back in Birmingham Charley decided, as Nur liked bus riding, they would go to Worcester to visit the cathedral. The bus was a single decker but that did not seem to reduce Nur's enjoyment. The cathedral was impressive and Nur was delighted when she saw King

John's tomb, which reminded her of her school history lessons. The cathedral was so huge and so old and she had a lot to tell Simon, her priest. Her other delight was sitting by the river while her husband had a beer and she tried a shandy. Luckily, this was a warm day with no rain, Charley had warned Nur that it often rained in England.

The next day the necklace was ready and Nur was surprised how light it felt. She wore a dark dress and that set off the sparkles coming from the diamond. All the men admired the setting and Nur had a perfect beauty to make the necklace look even better. Charley's mom was shocked by the diamond and asked how much it cost. Charley was not about to tell her. His grandfather and grandmother said they were in awe of the diamond and Nur was the perfect lady to show its full potential. Nur watched Charley with his mother and grandparents and could see how he responded to his family. Charley told them as they had an early flight they should not come to the airport. He was still feeling angry about his mother's attitude.

This was a long flight and Nur was very close to Charley and one of the stewardesses whispered to him that he should not try to escape. Charley was quietly laughing that a stranger had observed his good luck. The reception at Singapore airport was very happy with Aadam, Maryam, both brothers and Arthur present. Arthur and Jacob were dating two Chinese sisters and Arthur was very serious. They all went back to Aadam's house for dinner. Nur changed into a dark dress and put on the necklace. When she entered the dining room her mother immediately noticed it and screamed. Aadam looked at Charley and said, "Is that real?"

"Yes, we will tell you the story during dinner but I have known that stone for many years." They all crowded around Nur for a look and Aadam fetched his eye piece for a better look. Maryam came and gave Charley a kiss on the cheek that took him by surprise and made Nur smile. Her brothers were admiring this large diamond. Later Nur showed her mother her stockings and decided the only place she could wear them was in an air-conditioned hotel. She also told her about Carnaby Street and her mother was speechless.

The news from Hong Kong was all good. Trevor had a successful accounting company. Li's tailoring business was booming and short skirts were selling like hot cakes. Nur was very pleased with Li's success. The carvings were in high demand and the carver was working full time making carvings for Charley. Aadam was deciding what he could get from Italy that would sell in Singapore. Uncle Joshua wanted them to visit any time they could and Charley owed him money for wood so that they would have to go soon.

Charley booked seats on a train going north to Malaya and told Nur to pack her best dresses. Nur was surprised but she realised Charley wanted to impress her uncle. She was not too keen on flaunting her necklace but Charley insisted she show her aunt and uncle. She wore the necklace under her dress on the train and sat very close to Charley. At her uncle's house she kept it under her dress until the cousins were in bed. Uncle and aunty were suitably impressed when she finally revealed the stone from under her dress. Again, Charley was asked if the stone was real. Joshua was very interested in its history. Nur realised it was a burden and she wondered where she could wear it in public; Charley was also wondering when and where she could wear it. The crime rate in Singapore was very low but this stone would be a big temptation for any thief. Nur's aunt told her she had found a husband who was one in a million and was hoping her children could find suitable spouses. Marriage was very important and she would hold Nur as an example for her children.

Joshua had samples of several hard woods and Charley was keen to try them all. They discussed the origins of the wood; the Italian buyer seemed interested where these trees were grown. Joshua only had praise for Charley. Charley owed him money so he was writing a cheque when Joshua said he should rewrite it as Charley had spelt his name wrong.

"The banks are very sticky about names and you have spelt my name in the biblical way *Josua* but my name has an *h*. I think someone wrote the wrong name on my birth certificate. At school I was called Josh and so I never changed the spelling."

"I think that happened with me as I have seen my name without the *e* and even with an *ie* at the end."

They had a good laugh at the spellings of their names; Charley was happy that Joshua had his sense of humour. Joshua was keen to discuss the carving business as his American clients could not get enough. Charley told him to get his carvers to put *Malaya* in the carving. Joshua thought that a brilliant idea and he wanted to cut Charley in on the profits as he had stolen Charley's idea. Charley did not protest too much as his bank balance was low. Later in Singapore he met one of the students who had been on the taxation course. This man was an advisor to the government. He told him about the carvings and the man was very enthusiastic and said he would try to get Charley a government commendation.

A few months passed and one day Nur told Charley she might be pregnant. She watched as his face changed finally to a smile. He asked what they should do. She said they should book an appointment with a doctor. Charley had never seen a doctor in Singapore and was happy when Arthur told him of an Indian doctor who specialized in pregnancy. Nur had also never visited a doctor and was happy with Charley's choice. Charley had told Arthur to keep quiet about this development and certainly not tell Jacob.

The doctor examined Nur and put his stethoscope on her belly.

"There is nothing to be worried about but I would like you to have an ultrasound examination. It is fairly new and non-intrusive but will give us a better idea of what is going on in there."

Of course when a doctor tells you not to worry, you worry and Nur and Charley were no exceptions. They booked an appointment with a clinic. Archie was breathing heavily as they approached the clinic and he had a bad feeling. A young Chinese girl did the examination and Nur talked to her in Cantonese. The technician was very happy to see them, they were the first multinational couple she had treated.

"You definitely have a foetus but there may be a second. Come back in a month and the picture may be clearer."

Nur and Charley were speechless and Charley started to sweat. This was so unexpected and neither of them could think what to say. Charley was thinking one baby would be enough but now there might be two. How was Nur going to cope with two babies? Charley would probably be of no use. Expecting one child was good news but two could be a problem.

"Twins, my god twins" was all Charley could say.

"Let's not tell our parents until we are sure. I don't want them to get too excited and I have to get used to this development."

"How about me?"

Nur was the calming influence and that settled Charley's nerves. A month passed and twins were confirmed; one could be a boy. Charley was telling Nur to relax but he was the most nervous. At dinner Nur told her parents that she was pregnant. Maryam started screaming and Aadam calmed her. After a short while Nur said there was other news. The other news was that they were going to have twins. Aadam had no chance of calming his wife. Maryam was kissing Nur and Charley and dancing around the room. Aadam was getting out his best bottle of brandy; dinner was forgotten. Neither Aadam nor Maryam could think of twins in their family. Aadam thought that twins in Singapore were a rarity. He was going to investigate, he said he could not yet express his feelings; Maryam had no problem with her feelings, she kept shouting "Twins, thank the Lord."

Charley wrote to his grandfather and mother about the news. His grandfather replied that his sister had twins but one died in birth. Charley tried to hide that letter but Nur found it. She told Charley that medicine had progressed a lot since that time and he should not hide things from her as she was strong. His mother's reply was very positive and she said his auntie Ann had told her there were twins in his father's family. Now Nur jokingly told him it was all his fault. When Maryam found the family connection she would hug Charley every time she saw him.

Jacob and Arthur were very happy to congratulate them. Paul's congratulation was a little backhanded.

"Congratulations, but I don't think I can beat that."

Congratulations also came from Trevor and Li. As Li could not have children they were thinking of adopting. Uncle Joshua said that Charley and Nur were so special he would name his new company Charlnur after them. Nur insisted she would work until she was unable, her mother insisted they move into the family home; four flights were too much for a pregnant woman. Charley tried to dissuade Nur from working but he knew he was losing that argument. When the news was spread there were lots of visiting relatives. These visitors were often surprised that Nur was still working. Aadam left most of the entertaining to Maryam and Charley tried to be absent a lot of the time. He would often go the shop and have a beer with Jacob and Arthur. They sat outside watching the mayhem and several accidents. Arthur was telling Charley that he was totally at peace and would stay in Singapore forever. Jacob told Charley he would soon join uncle Joshua in business.

Another ultrasound confirmed there was a boy and a girl. Charley could not believe the photographs and Maryam almost fainted when she saw them. Aadam wanted to donate to the clinic, he had never seen such 'photos'. He sat and looked at them for a long time.

The babies were born and Charley sent a telegram to his mother. A return telegram said she was on her way. Charley was a bit surprised but Nur was very happy. Maryam wanted to be with the babies all the time. She would greet visitors but send them away saying the time was inconvenient. Aadam was very pleased but upset about the commotion he would be missing from the house for several hours.

Charley took Maryam to the airport to meet his mother. Charley was greeted by lots of kisses; Jill and Maryam were hugging and kissing. The ladies sat in the back seat as Charley drove them home. He was left in the car as the ladies swiftly entered the house. The cordiality between his mother and mother-in-law had surprised him and left him a bit lost. When he reached the sitting room his mother was kissing Nur and the babies. She had changed and Charley was on the back foot, not knowing quite what to do. He kissed his son, daughter and Nur and excused himself. He wanted to assess the situation; he had to have time alone. His mother's change in attitude had him thinking how to handle this new situation.

Later that evening he talked to Nur and found there had been a frank discussion. Jill told Nur she was jealous that another woman had taken her little Charley away. Jill's father had told her it was inevitable he would get married and have children. When news of the twins came she had changed her mind about the marriage. Apparently Maryam had congratulated Jill on being so open and being the mother of her favourite son. Maryam said she could understand that having only one child was a big burden and she was glad she had three.

The next day Maryam took Jill shopping to get some more suitable clothes. They had a great time and Maryam insisted on buying Jill a summer outfit. These two ladies were both changed and Maryam was telling Jill it was Charley who changed her and she was now very happy. The twins were something out of the ordinary and it was all due to Charley.

While the ladies were out Charley enjoyed the peace and quiet sitting with his wife and very sleepy babies. He told Nur he was a bit confused how to treat his mother. Nur was telling him that all the problems were behind them. Charley knew she was correct but he still had his doubts. When the ladies returned Jill approached her son and said she had only planned on staying two weeks but could she stay longer? Before Charley could answer, Maryam said, "You can stay here forever if you like."

Lionel

"I have been asked to send you to an arms training camp. I am not in favour of British police being armed but I agree some of us have to know how to use weapons. This will be an opportunity for you and I will not want you to miss it." This was the chief constable telling Lionel of his transfer.

Lionel had been born in a better suburb of Birmingham during the bombing. Actually in 1941 the bombing was not so bad and there were only a few stray bombs in his area. He went to a good infants' school followed by a good junior school. Lionel was leading a fairly sheltered life. Of course the war had ended but Lionel was able to catch a tram or a bus to see many bombed sites. These were not close to where he lived but he wanted to see what the German bombers had done. One bus took him to an area which had seen plenty of destruction. Ladywood was a very different area than Quinton; there were many factories but many bombs had hit residential areas. Lionel took all these sights to his class at school. His parents told him that he should think about the positives and not dwell on the negatives. They only wanted to believe that they had won the war and now everything was going to change for the better. All the children wanted to talk about the war but many of the teachers were not keen on talking about the worst time in their lives. Lionel's parents were also not keen on discussing the war.

At school Lionel was a good pupil and always top of his class. He was also good at sport and was a good runner. At home both parents encouraged him to try his best at everything. His junior school had a master who tutored in football and cricket. Lionel had a good eye and became proficient at batting. Cricket was only played with a tennis ball and not a hard cricket ball. His father took him to the park and showed him to throw. He was regularly playing football in the street, which was a cul-de-sac so there was very little traffic.

His mother was a well-educated lady and was secretary to the town planner. She always insisted Lionel write in his spare time. He was left handed and she bought him a biro. The old pen and ink were difficult for left handers. Both his mother and father were right handed. His father wrote a very nice copper plate script but slowly. His father had been to Catholic school and maybe forced to write right handed; Lionel was too polite to ask. Asking parents awkward questions was not the done thing. Lionel watched his father and he did many things with his left hand.

Lionel was approaching eleven and his mother was telling him he had to take the eleven plus and go to grammar school. Many of his school mates were scared of this test but Lionel was not fazed. He passed the test and was going to Handsworth Grammar School; that meant a bit of bus travel but he was not troubled. In his first class he met many other pupils from a wide area of Birmingham. Quite a few had different accents and he learned a few new words. The first year was non-selective going by alphabetical order of surnames. The second year they were selected by how well they had done in the first year exams. Lionel was always near the top of the class in all the years he was at school. What let him down was mathematics; there were always several others better than him. His mother always signed his year report but admitted she could not help him with mathematics because it was her weak subject.

At sport he was in the under-fifteen cross country team, the football team and the cricket team. He played cricket with the older boys and opened the batting. His teachers had noticed his abilities and wanted him to stay at school after sixteen; they wanted him to go into the sixth form. His father was less demanding than his mother and told him to make up his own mind when he had passed his O-levels. All his mother would tell him was that she was keen he should continue in education. Lionel was a bit bored with school and wanted to start work. An education adviser came to the school and suggested the police force. Lionel thought that was a good possibility, the more he thought about it and read some literature the more he liked the idea. He would be learning new things and that might satisfy his mother.

Lionel sat the O-level exam and received eight passes all in the top grade. His mother was very proud. She said he should go into the sixth form. He took a few weeks off and enjoyed his free time. He then signed up for the police force; his mother was not too pleased. She told him he could still join the police with A-levels and go in at a higher rank than constable. He became a police cadet and was taken to a camp and fitted for a uniform. At school he had been one of the tallest pupils but some of his fellow recruits were over six feet. There was a fair bit of marching and lots of lectures. Lionel found the lectures on the law most interesting. The admissibility of evidence and how to take evidence were an area he thought would be most useful. There was recreation and as it was summer he could use his skill to full advantage. This was the hard cricket ball and some of his fellow students were fast bowlers and trying to hit his head. He could bowl as well as bat and had many a batsman bamboozled by his spin bowling.

Lionel loved the first weeks and was not missing home. During the second week they were taken to the firing range. The instructor took small groups and showed them how to load different pistols. Some were old pistols from World War Two and several were German pistols. He then asked each man to pick a pistol and load it. Lionel picked a Luger as he liked the look and it fitted into his hand. The sergeant nodded that it was a good choice. Lionel was the only left hander in the group so the sergeant let him fire first. The rest of the group had their go but not one had the accuracy of Lionel. He had hit the bull five times and the first shot was on the edge of the bull. The sergeant asked Lionel to pick another gun. Lionel looked at the guns and picked a colt. He remembered the cowboy pictures at the cinema on a Saturday morning. His first shot was a bit off but hit the target. He adjusted and the next five shots hit the bull's eye. The sergeant dismissed the group and asked Lionel to stay back.

"Have you ever fired a pistol before?"

"No, sir, I have never handled any firearm, we had army cadets at school but I did not join."

"You were shooting with your arm extended. Could you shoot with a bent arm and the pistol close to your body?"

The sergeant demonstrated the position. Lionel did as he was told and hit the bull with all six shots. The sergeant said Lionel should report to him next week as he was going to be taken somewhere. Lionel had to write a report every day and this was the most interesting one. During the next week on a Thursday he was excused all other duties and met the sergeant who had commandeered a jeep.

The sergeant was a speedy driver and had Lionel taking deep breaths occasionally. They drove to a nearby army barracks. The sergeant told Lionel he would be shooting rifles on an army firing range. Lionel was quite excited although he tried not to show it. The army sergeant in charge of the range welcomed them.

The two sergeants knew each other well and after a brief chat the army sergeant addressed Lionel.

"I understand you are a new recruit. Would you like to ask any questions?"

"Yes, sir, I have never fired a rifle before so could I have a trial shot?"

"You certainly can, I will show you how to load this old Enfield 303 which I regard as the most accurate rifle we have. You will lie down and focus on the target and fire when you are ready. Just beware, the butt will give a kick when you fire."

Lionel's first shot hit the target but was just outside the bull's eye. He then reloaded, hit the bull and did the same with the next four shots. The army sergeant was amazed and asked again whether Lionel had shot a rifle before. He said that none of his recruits could shoot like that. He wanted them to come back the next week so Lionel could have an audience and some competition. The police sergeant asked Lionel to write a report as it would go on his record.

Lionel completed his course at the college and was back in Birmingham as an ordinary policeman. He was on foot patrol in the Jewellery Quarter and parts of Hockley. During the day the Jewellery Quarter was quiet but later a few of the pubs stayed open and they were lively. Hockley was never quiet and he had to try to break up a few fights. It seemed that most of the problem was between Irish groups and no one wanted to hurt a young copper. Lionel did not really understand the animosity between the groups.

At the weekend he joined a football team as a fill-in player he did not always know when he would be on duty. He did not tell them he was a policeman. During this time he became friendly with an Irish boy from Southern Ireland. This lad told Lionel he was glad he did not live in Hockley; he did not know that was where Lionel worked. They had a lot of discussion about the trouble in Ireland. Lionel learned a lot about the country.

Lionel did not really like night duty but there would be two of them if he had to work after nine as many of the pubs shut at ten p.m. On some nights before nine p.m. he would escort the Salvation Army ladies as they visited the pubs. It always amazed him that when these ladies entered the pub everything would quieten down and the patrons seemed to give generously to the shaking tins.

One evening he was in Hockley and was approaching two groups standing on either side of the road. He sensed there would be a problem and was going to get in between the two groups but he was too late. Someone shouted something about the Pope and from the other side came an insult about marching bands and it became an all-out brawl. They told Lionel to stay out of it. He blew his whistle and luckily there were two other policemen nearby. Their appearance calmed the situation as all the men had work the next day and did not want to be arrested. Lionel wrote a report and a long article about the problem between the Catholics and Protestants.

This report came to the attention of the chief constable and he read the report. He told his deputy that this young man was going to rise up in the force. He then looked into his cadet record and found that the firearms sergeant wrote that Lionel was the best shot he had ever seen. Coincidentally, other officers in London were reading Lionel's record. There was interest in setting up a special police squad who could be licensed to carry fire arms at all times. There was always the provision for police to apply to the courts to carry arms but at this time it was not common. Many in the police force were against police carrying arms; they thought that most problems could be solved by professional use of the truncheon.

This new force asked the Chief Constable to interview Lionel and see whether he was interested in joining an elite unit. It was impressed on the chief that the utmost secrecy should be maintained. Lionel was called to the chief constable's office and asked if he would like to go to London to join a special force. If he refused there would be nothing on his record. Whether he accepted or declined the offer he was not allowed to say anything to other police and his parents. This unit was not part of the London Metropolitan Force and would be a special armed squad. Lionel thought for a very short time and agreed to join.

He told his parents he was being transferred to a unit in London to get more experience. His mother asked lots of questions. She was worried there was more crime in London. He told her he would probably have a lot of desk work as he had to understand the system. He would probably not have to go out on foot patrol. His mother was satisfied and his father was telling him to take any opportunity that was available. Actually, Lionel was not sure what he would be doing.

The commander was a young fellow with the rank of Chief Superintendent. He preferred to be called Commander. Initially there would be a unit of twenty five men and they would train with all kinds of weapons. He stressed they should learn about the accuracy and the reliability of each weapon. They should learn about silencers and how they worked. It was important to know what weapon and what bullet to use in each situation. The main thing to learn was when to shoot and when not to shoot. And, if required to shoot what part of the target to hit; these twenty five men were good shots. Most times just showing the weapon could act as a deterrent but not always. They would see films of other police forces using their weapons and they had to analyze each situation. One other important topic was to learn how to write reports which were always required and should only contain facts.

Lionel loved this approach and wanted to learn as much as he could.

After watching several films of armed police in certain situations the Commander told them as they were not in these films he wanted their opinions and observations. The first and most powerful film was of the recent Sharpeville massacre in South Africa, where black policemen shot black demonstrators. Another film showed police in Cyprus keeping apart Greek and Turkish demonstrators with batons and shields; although they were armed they did not use their firearms. A third film showed a crowd harassing police. The film was in Spanish with subtitles; Lionel thought it might be in Mexico. The police commander warned the protesters that his men were armed and they would shoot if they had to do. He then told two policemen to fire over the crowd's heads and warned the next shots would be lower; the crowd dispersed.

The commander read each report and called each man to discuss their reports. He called in Lionel and bade him sit down.

"First, I liked your reports. You were the only one to have a title and that told me how you felt about the film. For the Sharpeville film you had *overkill;* for the Cyprus film you had *no shooting needed* and for the Spanish one you had *wise warning*. I really did not need to read the reports as you had told me what I wanted to know in the title. You did bring out an important point in the Sharpeville film which I had not thought much about. Were the black policemen a different tribe than the protestors? I don't have the answer and I will try to find out. Bravo! I give you top marks for these reports."

Lionel left the office with a broad beam on his face. He had tried to condense his reports into two pages but he could have written more and bored the commander. The films had made a lasting impression on Lionel and he wrote longer reports for himself.

After the initial training each man was sent to a different constabulary. Reports should be sent to the Commander every week. The commander told Lionel as he was the youngest and probably the best shot, initially, he would be kept in London and assigned to an East End station. He would just be a normal constable but he would be allowed to carry his gun although it should be concealed. In winter his great coat would be good covering but in summer he had to make his own judgment how he carried his pistol.

Lionel reported to a superintendent who assigned him his duties. He would be on foot patrol in the Mile End Road area. During day time he would be alone but on night patrol he would accompany another constable. The superintendent hoped he would not have to use his firearm but if his life was threatened the superintendent would support him at the inevitable enquiry. The general area had lots of petty crime and some racially motivated related violence but the real problem was drugs. There were known gangs in the area but in general they did not threaten police although where drugs were concerned thing were getting nasty.

Lionel enjoyed his patrol, he was able to go wherever he chose, most East Enders were very friendly. In any shop he entered he was greeted and treated politely. During the summer he would visit one or two of the pubs for a glass of lemonade to quench his thirst and always made sure he paid for his drink. The landlords were very friendly and he was never abused in a pub. Night patrol was more exciting as there was often trouble at pub closing times. Two constables showing up generally quelled the situation and they only had to use their truncheons a couple of times; Lionel never had to use his pistol. Each incident was reported to the commander who was considering moving Lionel to a new location.

There was one unpleasant duty in the East End and that was arresting 'methos'. There was a small group of men who drank anything they could get their hands on including methylated spirits. Lionel knew one of their hangouts and he tried to tell them they would go blind. These men were homeless, dirty and smelly and they had lost all hope. They seemed to believe that diluting the 'meths' with water or pop reduced the blinding effect. The laboratories of a couple of local schools and colleges had been broken into and this group was suspected but with no evidence they could not be arrested. There were always two on night patrol and one night as they were passing a school they heard breaking glass. Lionel's mate went towards the sound while Lionel made for the other side of the school. He heard his mate shout stop and then a door opened on Lionel's side of the building.

Out shuffled a scruffy old man (probably not that old) and tried to run away but Lionel quickly caught up with him. Lionel shouted to stop but the man kept on running, if you could call it that. Lionel really did not want to touch him so he tapped his ankle with his truncheon. The man stumbled and fell throwing a bottle away as he fell. It turned out the bottle contained methylated spirits. The 'metho' was escorted to the station with Lionel able to avoid touching him. The man would at least have a bath and a warm cell where he could sleep.

One day when he was on patrol he was passing through a market when one of the stall holders quietly told him there were drugs being sold in a side street nearby. Lionel walked down this street and he saw a man pass a package to another man. Lionel rushed up and grabbed the dealer. He had this man by the collar when he was confronted by three men. They were probably his bodyguards.

"Let him go."

"No, he is under arrest for drug dealing so get out of the way I am taking him to the station, you can come if you wish."

"You are going nowhere."

Lionel realised he would have to draw his gun to even up the odds. These men were blocking his path.

"My preferred weapon is this Luger and I am a good enough shot to shoot any part of your body I wish. Now please get lost before I have to waste a bullet. Bullets cost money."

The three men disappeared and Lionel was able to escort the dealer to the station in front of an appreciative market crowd. Several packets of a white powder were found on the suspect. The superintendent was very happy and a smiling commander read an extensive report. The superintendent was very glad Lionel had not had to fire his weapon but could see the advantage of the gun as a deterrent. The commander decided that Lionel should go outside of a big city so his new assignment was in rural Devon. This time he would be in a police patrol vehicle.

Lionel met the chief constable of the area who was not in favour of armed police but he did warn that many farmers had registered firearms mainly shotguns. Lionel was lodged in a police house with three other constables. One was a good cook and that was good news to Lionel. They were all interested in his Luger but they all said there was no need for it in this area. So far there were few drugs and almost no armed robberies in Devon. Most of the time, Lionel was in the car stopping vehicles without licences or tax certificates. There were a couple of fights in pubs at closing times but it always seemed to be holiday makers. He was enjoying living in Devon, a place his family would often go for holidays. The local people were friendly and during his time off he enjoyed visiting some coastal villages with one of his buddies doing the driving. He was taking driving lessons although he was still a bit young but had special permission to hold a licence.

While on patrol they got a call about a farmer mistreating his wife. The wife had called in and asked for help. They were very close to the property and as they approached the farmhouse they were confronted by the farmer shouting for them to leave his property as he was armed. Lionel called the chief constable and asked if he would bring a rifle. The chief was a little put out by this request but brought the rifle. He then insisted they negotiate with the farmer. Lionel agreed as the rifle was a last resort. Negotiations went on for several hours without anything happening. It was starting to get dark and finally the chief constable asked for Lionel's opinion.

"There is a large window in the front room and a ceiling light behind that window. I will first shoot out the window and then the light. The man will know we mean business and know we have a marksman."

"I just hope he does not look through that window."

"Don't worry, sir, I will hit the top of the pane and unless he is a giant he will not be hurt except maybe from flying glass. Do I have your permission?"

Lionel did what he said he would do after he had permission. Within one minute the man emerged with his hands held high. His wife followed shouting to the police that they should not shoot her husband. In the chief constable's office Lionel was given a glass of single malt whiskey. The chief constable admitted that there was a place for firearms used properly and he would get one or two men in his force trained in their use. The commander was highly delighted at that report. He was now getting reports that some other area commands were considering arming some police personnel. He was also thinking of arming some police women.

Lionel's next assignment was Northern Ireland. The commander had read Lionel's early report about Hockley and the warring Irishmen. Lionel was going to Belfast and a police force dominated by protestant Northern Irishmen. Lionel was remembering his Southern Irish football friend and was worried about his emotions. He was hoping he could keep quiet and view the situation with an open mind. The commander told him to be impartial; he was there to observe and keep his opinions to himself.

He arrived in Belfast to a good welcome, he was known as a hot shot. Lionel was worried about that title, he might have to prove it. Most of his fellow policemen were armed and so he was not alone. The superintendent took him to the firing range to assess Lionel's expertise. After his six shots the superintendent said he would call on Lionel in special situations. Lionel spent a lot of time in the office learning about the situation in Northern Ireland; the enemy was the IRA. Marching bands close to or entering Catholic areas were always causing confrontations. Lionel kept his opinions to himself and just tried to be an impartial observer as he had been instructed. Whenever they were on patrol in a Catholic area he could feel the tension. He did not like this assignment and that probably came through to his commander. He was about to be transferred when a situation arose. He was with the superintendent when there was a riot. The police line was confronted by a crowd throwing rocks, then a Molotov cocktail was thrown followed by a second. The superintendent asked if Lionel could put that thrower out of action. Lionel shot the man in the shoulder and said he could be arrested when he would surely go to hospital. The superintendent was very pleased as the crowd then dispersed. He said he would let Lionel go back to England as his identity might be known; he would then be a marked man.

Back in England his commander was very pleased and so far Lionel had made a good impression wherever he went. His next assignment was going to be an international one. He was off to North America to observe the police forces of Mexico, America and Canada.

He had two weeks' leave while he obtained a passport with the required visas. He went home to Birmingham to stay with his parents. He was very quiet about his duties and his mother was asking when he would be promoted. His father was easier, he was only interested in whether Lionel would stay in the force. He told them he was going to North America to observe other police forces. His mother thought that was an excellent sign for possible promotion.

Lionel flew to Mexico City and was met by a chief inspector of the federal police. There was a cursory look at his passport and a stamp. There was no customs check and he was whisked away to the federal police headquarters. The inspector, Miguel, spoke excellent English as he had spent many years in the United States and he was keen to see Lionel shoot. Lionel had no chance to get over jet lag and was escorted to the firing range and presented with a good choice of weapons.

He was amazed at the guns available in the armoury. The sergeant in charge was inviting him to pick any weapon. He picked a Luger and Miguel nodded approvingly. At the firing range Lionel showed his skill and Miguel and the sergeant in charge were clapping his every shot. Back in Miguel's office Lionel was told that his record had preceded him. Miguel was keen to have contact with the British police; he admitted he did not really like the American police. He had spent time in Texas and he wanted to go to London. Miguel said Lionel must be hungry so they would go to his apartment where Lionel would be staying. Lionel was hungry as he had only eaten breakfast on the plane.

Miguel's place was a large three bedroomed apartment in the centre of Mexico City. Lionel was greeted by Miguel's wife Mary and three young children. The food was delicious; he tried mango for the first time and loved it. The family watched him eat and then they wanted Lionel to tell them about England. He told them about Birmingham and London. The children were so enthralled Mary had a problem to send them to bed. What intrigued them most was that most police officers were unarmed and only had a whistle and a truncheon.

Mary said to Miguel, "We have to go live in England."

The next day Miguel explained the Mexican police system which was complex and susceptible to change at any time. Often the police and the military were quite close and the politicians were always interfering. Mexico City had a high crime rate and many of the criminals were armed. Drugs and prostitution were the main problems with gangs having frequent turf wars. Lionel was assigned to a police car with a sergeant who spoke English and two constables who spoke no English. Lionel would carry his Luger and the others would be armed. A submachine gun would be in the car and other weapons in the trunk. Miguel thought he should have called it the boot. They would patrol the southern perimeter of the city. Miguel warned that there were many shanty towns and unless they had reinforcements their car would not enter such areas. Lionel was not used to no-go areas.

He was introduced to the sergeant who spoke good English; he had lived in Acapulco. He was introduced to the two constables who seemed to be bowing to him.

Lionel greeted them in English and shook their hands. He sat in the back with one of the constables and off they went. The first few days they were just pulling over cars driven erratically and picking up drunks on the side of the road. Lionel had not needed to draw his Luger once. Back in Miguel's flat they could not get enough of Lionel's stories. It was the same in the headquarters, he was answering many questions. He told them about fogs and they were telling him Mexico City had fogs. He told them about coal fires and tin baths (he had never used one). Lionel was a celebrity and whenever he spoke he could hear translations in the background. These police were very friendly and he was getting admiring looks from some young policewomen.

He was assigned for one month in Mexico and the time was passing very fast. They were on the highway south of the city when the sergeant who was driving saw a vehicle he thought was stolen. They pulled over the car to check the licence and registration; they were not expecting a problem. As the two constables approached the car the driver emerged and pulled out a pistol. The constables had not drawn their weapons and stopped. Lionel had drawn his pistol as he was not sure what was happening. He shot the pistol from the man's hand and the driver stood with his arm by his side and his hand dripping blood. The sergeant was out of the car in a shot with his gun pointing at the car. The two constables now had their guns drawn. Lionel had made an instant decision and had a clear line of fire.

In the back seat of the car there were two women who did not move. The sergeant took control and said one of the officers would drive the car and Lionel should have his Luger drawn to watch the women. They would not be examined (he used the word frisked) and they could be armed. The injured man would be taken to hospital and then brought in for questioning. As they entered the car the constable said something to the women which Lionel could not understand. At the station Lionel was a hero; one female officer came up and kissed him. The sergeant came and there was a lot of shaking hands. The constable told the sergeant what he had said to the women. The sergeant was laughing. Lionel asked what had been said because these women were very quiet; they never moved.

The sergeant told Lionel the constable had said, "He can shoot off both of your nipples before you feel the pain."

Lionel thought that was probably impossible but it worked as those two ladies were scared to move. Miguel was very happy but he was unhappy that Lionel was leaving in two days. Back in the apartment Mary and the children all gave him a kiss. They had fed him very well with spicy food to his liking. Lionel had enjoyed his time in Mexico and never had the chance to try all the automatic weapons available. As he was leaving he joined a queue as directed by Miguel. Lionel was not sure what was going on but just obeyed orders. When they came to the desk a sergeant rose, saluted, and stamped a card which he gave to Lionel.

Miguel said, "That is your release from the Mexican Federal Police you don't really need it but it will remind you of these past weeks."

Lionel thought he would definitely remember these weeks. He was escorted to the airport; there was a stamp in his passport and no other formalities. He was taken to the plane by Miguel who said, "It has been a pleasure to have you with us and I hope we will meet again back here or maybe in London."

He now was off to Dallas, Texas and he had to show his shooting expertise. They wanted him to wear an American revolver as they were not keen on the Luger. He was again assigned to traffic control and noticed every time a vehicle was pulled over the constables had their weapons drawn before they left the patrol car. Frisking suspects was often a violent operation. Lionel was not keen on this kind of policing. His second posting was to rural Iowa and a very different place to police. In a small town in Iowa the sheriff told him there had only been one bank robbery in twenty years and that was ten years ago. Lionel stayed above the local pub and there was no problem at closing time; everyone knew each other. The major crimes in this town were children's bicycles being stolen (borrowed) by other children and underage drinking.

He never saw a policeman draw his gun but once when they pulled over a car with Illinois plates the sheriff had his hand on his gun as he approached the vehicle. The sheriff was a jovial man seemingly liked by the town's people. He had a rule that when teenagers were caught drinking if the local football team had won they had a caution and if they had lost they had a fine. This was apparently a town ordinance voted in by the voters. Lionel learned to relax in this town, all the conversations were about barbecued steak, farming, corn and black soil.

Next he was off to Buffalo, a big city in New York State. The police chief welcomed him and told him about the problems of crime in the city. He noticed that most of the petty crime was blamed on the black population and the major crime blamed on crime gangs from New York City. He got to know there were many Poles and other Eastern Europeans in the city; they had tasty food. When he got to talk to them it was all about the problems with the blacks. It was a problem to talk to black residents but he visited some shops and when they realised he was not American they talked to him. They felt they were always being harassed by the police.

One constable in the police car told Lionel about his private arsenal at home. The man had two Colt revolvers, a shotgun and a semi-automatic weapon. He also had pepper spray and he said he had the right to bear arms under the constitution. This obsession with guns bewildered Lionel who thought it was close to madness. Lionel was glad when his time was up and he was going to Canada. He thought maybe his time in

Iowa had allowed him to relax between the stress of Texas and Buffalo.

He was taken across into Canada via the bridge at Niagara Falls. What he saw of the falls was impressive but he thought it was better on film. He was picked up by two RCMP constables (Royal Mounted Police). They had no horses but a speedy car. He was whisked off to Toronto to their Ontario headquarters. Again he was asked to show his shooting prowess. He was issued with a Glock pistol and warned only to use it in the most extreme circumstance. The pistol would be in a holster with a flap that needed to be undone before the pistol could be extracted. Lionel was warned that RCMP officers rarely drew their guns.

The next few days Lionel spent in their library studying the complexity of Canadian policing. Besides the RCMP there were provincial police and municipal police in large cities. Very few incidents involved shots being fired. The RCMP had a 'hit' squad in each province, these officers had normal duties and could be called on if there was a violent demonstration; they could also be used as snipers. The RCMP had less involvement in normal policing in Ontario and Quebec where the provisional police were responsible for most of the police work. Lionel was able to travel to Ottawa to see the ceremonial duties of the RCMP; he thought he would love to dress in their uniform.

From Ottawa he was sent to Regina in Saskatchewan, where the RCMP were trying to intercept drug shipments from the US. The borders with Montana, North Dakota and Minnesota were very porous. Lionel was assigned to a patrol car operating south of Regina stopping many US licence-plated cars. His three colleagues told him the smugglers tried to get hold of Canadian plated vehicles but many were in too much of a hurry. He saw many cars stopped and two drug 'busts' but only saw pistols drawn once. They had tried to stop a car with Canadian plates that was being driven erratically. They finally pulled it over and two police approached with pistols drawn; Lionel had his pistol drawn just in case. The driver turned out to be intoxicated but there was an unlicensed firearm in the vehicle.Noshotswerefired.

Lionel was then sent to Lethbridge, Alberta which is very close to the US border. For some reason the town seemed to be flooded with American cigarettes with no duty paid. The RCMP thought that this might be an offshoot of the drug trade. Lionel was with three other officers when they raided a shop. Although guns were not drawn each man had his hand on his holster. The RCMP had a tip-off and in the back room they found illegal cigarettes and marijuana.

The chief constable was very pleased with this find but he thought this was not organized crime but a small band of lower level criminals. What really excited him was something Lionel had noticed. As the other officers searched the back room Lionel was told to watch the owner who seemed to be nervous about his counter and not taking any notice of the officers searching the back room. Lionel moved behind the counter and the owner moved towards a drawer. Lionel pulled out his pistol and told the man to stand still; he thought there might be a firearm in the drawer. When he opened it he saw several passports and a lot of bank notes. They called for backup and an inspector came with three other constables. The inspector wore gloves as he examined the passports and the money and praised Lionel for not touching the evidence. These passports turned out to be forged and some of the money was also forged. Fingerprints were obtained from the evidence and the chief constable was bouncing with joy. Lionel and his colleagues had a boozy afternoon in the chief constable's office.

Lionel was happy in Lethbridge but he had to leave after a couple of months. He was flown to Vancouver where he met the deputy commissioner. This officer was full of praise for Lionel; they had smashed a major crime ring. The commissioner had always thought Lethbridge a bit of a backwater but Lionel had proved him wrong. The commissioner apologized for not having a medal for Lionel but the RCMP did not give out many medals. Lionel took a flight home from Vancouver to London where he was met by the commander. The reports from Lionel's tour were all glowing but the commander wanted Lionel to submit his reports.

Lionel sat in the office and put all his notes together and wrote three reports. He was reliving his experience in these reports and wishing he could do it all over again.

Mexico, he reported, was a federal police force continually changing by political decisions and his title was *a force we should support and help*.

The USA was a police force too willing to use firearms; his title *excessive use of force*.

Canada had a seeming reluctance to use firearms that might change in future; his title was *a police force that should have the greatest respect*.

The commander loved these reports and passed them up his chain of command. There was one article that gave him much pleasure. Lionel was good at reading and understanding news articles and quoting them in his reports. In this report a policeman on a motor cycle in Detroit saw two men exiting a shop with someone shouting, 'Stop thief'. While on his vehicle he drew his gun and shot one of the men dead. The other stopped and was arrested. The local newspapers were full of praise for the policeman and there was a very superficial enquiry. In a similar incident in Canada a policeman was on foot patrol when two men exited a shop while the owner was trying to restrain them. The officer ordered them to stop but one man kept running. The officer chased and fired above the man's head six times and then had to reload his pistol. Unfortunately the man tried to jump a fence as the seventh shot hit him in the head.

There was an extensive enquiry and the officer was stood down for over a month. Finally the officer was exonerated but this showed how the use of firearms by the police was viewed in the US and Canada.

The commander kept Lionel in London reading the reports of his fellow officers. Lionel was a bit embarrassed to point out mistakes in some reports but the commander said these details were confidential and Lionel should not worry. Many of the commands were considering having a few armed officers but the Birmingham command seemed reluctant. Lionel was sent back to Birmingham to talk to the chief constable.

Back there, his parents were very keen to hear his stories. His mother was a bit upset that he had not yet been promoted. Lionel had to hide his Luger, he was worried his mother might find it; he was not too worried about his father finding the gun. He had several chats with the chief constable. He was not trying to convince his superior but talking about his experiences. He was assigned to a police car patrolling the Ladywood area but often venturing towards the city centre. He loved this duty seeing areas of Birmingham with which he was not entirely familiar.

They had a call that there was a disturbance at the Birmingham Ice Rink; this was in their patrol area. They arrived to find a crowd outside being harangued by a man. As Lionel's partner approached the man he pulled out a large knife and then lunged at Lionel's mate. The lunge came close but Lionel's colleague backed off sufficiently so the knife did not touch him. As the man tried a second lunge Lionel shot him in the wrist and the knife dropped to the floor. The crowd started cheering and clapping. No one had cameras or mobile phones and so Lionel, his mate and the arrested man could escape without a positive identification. The newspapers got hold of the story and were headlining a hotshot in the police force. There was an internal enquiry in which Lionel explained he was not close enough to apprehend the man with the knife. The second lunge was probably going to result in his partner being stabbed. His partner backed up Lionel's observation. Lionel also told the inquiry that there were no people behind the man, only a brick wall. Lionel was exonerated but the chief constable wanted him to return to London before his identity was known.

"I would like you to stay here but when the publicity dies down you can come back."

As Lionel was leaving the chief constable told him he was having a rethink about armed police and the only reason to transfer Lionel was to get him out of the media attention. His mother knew nothing of the shooting but was dismayed he was going back to London. Lionel tried to explain he was learning all the time and there was so much to learn. In the morning he was picked up by an unmarked car with the driver in civvies; Lionel was also in civvies. They headed for the M1 but as they entered the motorway their car was clipped by a lorry in the slow lane. The car smashed into a bridge. The passenger side took the impact on the concrete support and Lionel was killed instantly.

The chief constable took it on himself to tell Lionel's parents of his death. Lionel's mother was in shock and all she could say was "what a sodding waste."

She did not normally swear but then she kept repeating the phrase over and over. Lionel's dad sought the advice of their doctor who explained she might be having a mental breakdown. The commander took Lionel's dad for a chat in the local pub; Lionel's mother could not understand what was going on. The commander explained Lionel's career and that he was soon to be promoted. He said he would arrange a guard of honour at the church. Lionel's father thanked him and he went to see the vicar of the church where the funeral would be held. He told the vicar that in his eulogy he might have a swear word. The vicar understood and said that would be okay.

The coffin was carried by four armed police men. Twenty others formed a guard of honour with rifles crossed above their heads.

Lionel's mother said, 'Who are these people?"

"They are here to pay their respects to our son, they are his colleagues."

Lionel had previously requested cremation although his mother wanted him to be buried. The commander told the congregation of Lionel's shooting prowess and some of his journey in the police force. He also said there were felicitations from a Mexican officer currently in London on secondment. There were also commiserations from a sheriff in rural Iowa.

Lionel's father talked about Lionel's early life. He was not too keen when Lionel joined the police force but Lionel had made it his career and excelled. He and his wife were both very proud of their only son. Finally, his father said, "All I can say is what his mother keeps saying; 'what a sodding waste!'"